ACCOLADES FOR CHRYSTAL GILKEY'S
A WISP OF FAITH

Chrystal Gilkey delivers a timely story that can help us grow spiritually in these uncertain times.

—Dr. J.D. Weido, pastor

An anonymous email request about a mysterious cloud launches a young meteorologist on a journey of discovery that will turn her wisp of faith into something much stronger. If you enjoy mystery and a sweet romance framed in a Christian worldview, don't miss *A Wisp of Faith* by Chrystal Gilkey.

—H.L. Wegley, author of
Voice in the Wilderness

In her first book, author Chrystal Gilkey skillfully narrates a suspenseful novel about a mysterious cloud in the town of Shady Springs and protagonist Mercedes' investigation of it. In her efforts to understand the cloud and the town's history, Mercedes will discover romance but also danger. Imminently enjoyable and written from a faith standpoint, be sure to read *A Wisp of Faith*!

—Michael B. Metts, PhD, co-author of *Jesus,
Skepticism, and the Problem with History*

Keep holding on,

A WISP OF

Faith

A Christian Novel

CHRYSTAL J. GILKEY

AUTHOR elite
ACADEMY

Chrystal Gilkey
Hebrews 10:23

Published by Author Academy Elite
PO Box 43, Powell, OH 43065
www.AuthorAcademyElite.com

Identifiers:
LCCN: 2021909179
ISBN: 978-1-64746-804-0 (paperback)
ISBN: 978-1-64746-805-7 (hardback)
ISBN: 978-1-64746-806-4 (ebook)

Available in paperback, hardback, e-book, and audiobook

Dedication

This book is dedicated to my children: Carley, Liam, and Finlee. With a little bit of faith in God, anything is possible!

Thy mercy, O Lord, is in the heavens; and thy faithfulness reacheth unto the clouds.

Psalms 36:5 (KJV)

1

MERCEDES

Sometimes, a wisp of faith is all we have to hold on to.

—Gertie

Mercedes Lewis enjoyed the muted tones of cocoa in her mocha coffee as she gazed at the sunset out her office window. Some may think of coffee as just a morning beverage, but for her, coffee was an all-day affair. Brilliant hues of gold and pink flooded the sky with intermittent wisps of clouds. At seven years old, Mercedes Lewis fell in love with clouds. She would swing for hours in her backyard, trying to reach high enough to grasp a little piece of heaven. Her mother always said she had her head in the clouds and even bought her a membership to the Cloud Appreciation Society for her twelfth birthday. Mercedes remembered opening the package as soon as it arrived, complete with a badge, membership card, certificate, and cloud identifier. She had worn the badge every day for several years. To this day, it remained her favorite gift. In fact, she still carried the membership card in her wallet.

It seemed only natural that she would go on to study weather (which turned out to be a more rigorous field than she anticipated) and receive her bachelor of science in meteorology. Mercedes finally felt like everything was coming together when she got her first job in broadcasting at the local news station a few months prior. Even sharing her office with two other coworkers couldn't dampen her excitement of one day being a lead meteorologist.

Mercedes glanced at her laptop, finally able to focus on the bizarre message she had received earlier that morning.

Dear Ms. Lewis,

I am from the town of Shady Springs, Arkansas. Our town has had a mysterious weather occurrence that has been going on for years. They say our town got its name from a cloud that sits over the lake. The cloud never leaves. Storms may move thru but after they've passed the cloud remanes. We would love someone to come and study it and see what scientific explain'n could be behind it. Also, our cloud seems to be getting smaller. Please come as soon as posible.

Signed,
A big fan and concerned citizen

The validity of the letter—full of typos and misspellings—and its author were questionable. It could be a child's prank. But it also could've been from someone who was simply unlearned in grammar and spelling. Mercedes might have dismissed the email entirely if it had not included a picture of the cloud. After enhancing the photograph, she recognized the formation as a lenticular cloud. *At least he's not trying to convince me he's seen a UFO like most do when they see a lenticular cloud.* North Arkansas did have some mountain-like terrain where lenticular clouds could theoretically form.

Mercedes typed the name of the town in her internet browser and pulled up an aerial view of the location, which revealed the land elevated and heavily forested. Shady Springs was about two hours southwest of Little Rock. She had never heard of the town before. Since the town was located out west, she didn't pass through on her drive to her hometown of El Dorado. She located Shady Springs on satellite, and sure enough, she saw a cloud hovering over the small lake.

Mercedes printed off the email and satellite to show her boss. Perhaps he would know what to make of it. As she headed out the door to find him, she bumped into the man she was on her way to visit, Reggie Thompson. Mercedes adored her boss. Short in stature, his reddish hair and Irish roots earned him plenty of leprechaun quips, which he handled good-naturedly. He moved with an air of energy contagious to those around him. Reggie Thompson was highly sought after in his field, yet he remained humble. He would remind his protégés, "The atmosphere always has a surprise for you." Mercedes eagerly anticipated their team meetings as a chance to glean whatever wisdom she could gain from the man.

Reggie's demeanor that day seemed unusually quiet. Mercedes felt a quiver of unease as he shut the door behind him.

Thirty minutes later, Reggie left the office for Mercedes to pack her things. Unforeseen cutbacks at the news station meant that since she was the last hire, she was the first to go. Reggie promised her a glowing reference, but it did little to soothe the shock and disappointment of his dismal disclosure. Mercedes blinked back tears as she put the few belongings she had kept in her shared office in an empty copy paper box.

"Well, Lord, what am I supposed to do now?" Mercedes wondered out loud. *Seriously?* A little voice inside mocked. *You haven't prayed in years, and you think now He is going to hear you? Because now you need him?*

Tears welled in her eyes at the nasty tone, which she quickly wiped away. Truthfully, she hadn't prayed or even thought about the Lord in a long time. When Mercedes was a teenager, her family began to go to church. She trusted the Lord as her Savior at fourteen years old and had a strong fire for the Lord. She even played the piano for some of their church services.

As Mercedes grew older, she felt deceived by different people in the church. Betrayals of trust and snarky critics made church the last place she wanted to be. Determined never again to be that vulnerable, Mercedes built a fortress around her heart. She was never going to let anyone have that much power or sway over her again. No one would ever make her feel worthless. Soon afterward, she went away for college and threw herself into her studies. She even stopped going to church and reading her Bible.

Why should God listen to my prayers? Why should He care about me? I certainly haven't done anything to deserve His attention.

The familiar soundtrack, "Concerning Hobbits (The Shire)," cut through her somber thoughts, and she knew it was her mother calling. They both had loved *The Lord of the Rings*. As the happy, Irish whistle melody and strings began to play, Mercedes answered. If anyone could lift her spirits, it would be her mother.

"Hey, Mom, hang on a minute. I'm stepping out the door!" Mercedes grabbed her box and purse and scurried out of her office for the last time. She didn't want to be caught by her office mates and lose her composure in front of them.

Alone in her apartment, Mercedes picked at the taco salad she'd made herself for dinner while she reflected on the conversation with her mother. Janet Lewis did not disappoint her "cheer mom" persona. She tried to persuade her daughter her unemployment was a "short hiatus," and the Lord was opening a door to something new and better. Of course, her mom also wanted her to come home for a visit and to work on resumés and such.

As much as she loved her mom, Mercedes did not want to go home. And as for God's plan for her life, Mercedes still didn't feel like He had an interest in her. When she prayed, she felt empty. She knew she couldn't base her faith on her feelings, but in her heart, it was hard to continue on with such disparity.

Done with her dinner, Mercedes began to go through her things from the office. Among her belongings, she found the email printout from earlier. She reread it and researched the town again on her phone. Shady Springs didn't have much going on, just a B&B and a couple of places to eat. They didn't even have Walmart, a staple in most Arkansas towns.

Her phone pinged, and she pulled up a text from her mom. *Getting your room ready, just in case!*

Mercedes sighed and skimmed over the email again. If a story happened to be there, it could help her career out. She sent a text back to her mom. *I am going to come visit, but I think I am going to stop at a town along the way and do a little weather investigation.*

Weather investigation? That sounds mysterious. What town?

Had her mother heard of the town? *Shady Springs, have you been there?*

She smiled as she read her mom's response. *Never have. Please call me when you get there! When are you leaving?*

She answered quickly to reassure her mother. *Okay, I will! Leaving sometime tomorrow.*

Mercedes pulled up the only hotel in Shady Springs on her phone and clicked the link to reserve a room. One bedroom, two nights, and sixteen digits of her credit card later, Mercedes felt like she had one thing accomplished. She went into her bedroom and sprawled out on her feather-top comforter, staring at the ceiling until her phone rang. She didn't recognize the number but answered anyway.

"Hello?" Mercedes closed her eyes; a stress headache began to throb across her temple.

"Hello, is this Mercedes Lewis?" an elderly lady's voice answered back.

"Yes, it is," Mercedes replied, picking at a string on her comforter.

"Good evening, Mrs. Lewis! My name is Gertie, and I own the Shady Springs B&B. I am calling to see what time you plan on arriving tomorrow. I wanted your room to be all ready for you."

Mercedes tried to think quickly. She hadn't even planned her departure. "Well, honestly, I'm not sure. Most definitely after lunch sometime."

"That's perfectly fine, dear." Gertie paused. "You wouldn't happen to be the meteorologist, Mercedes Lewis, would you?"

"Yes, ma'am, that's me." Mercedes prayed Gertie wouldn't ask her about her job.

"How wonderful! My sister is a big fan. We will see you tomorrow, dear, alright?"

"Yes, ma'am. See you then." Mercedes rolled off her bed to pack and began to rummage through her drawers for clothes for her adventure. Springtime in Arkansas required lots of layers because of its cold mornings and hot, humid afternoons.

After she packed, she fixed herself a cup of steaming hot English breakfast tea. As she lay in bed sipping her tea, she tried to relax and watch a show on BBC. *Why couldn't I live in a country with a designated teatime? Scones and crumpets are just my thing.* Actually, she wasn't really sure what a crumpet was, but it had to be good. On a whim, Mercedes searched "crumpets" on her phone. They didn't look too hard to make. *Might be fun to try and make with mom when I go home.* Unable to concentrate on the show, she turned off the television and drifted into a restless sleep.

The next morning, Mercedes lazed around in bed, surfing social media and drinking coffee. Her phone rang. Her heart skipped a beat when she saw Reggie's name. Perhaps there had been a mistake, and she still had a job? Eagerly, she accepted the call.

Her heart sank when Reggie said he was only calling to check in on her. She thanked him for calling and told him about her trip, to which he seemed interested, and asked for an update if she discovered anything.

As soon as she ended the call, her office mate, Kimberly, rang and lamented her situation. "It should have been Tucker," Kimberly scoffed angrily. "He is such a weasel." Mercedes was inclined to agree with her. Tucker, their other office mate, wanted to be on top and would mow down anyone in his way. On more than one occasion, he had tried to sabotage Mercedes, but she always managed to pull through.

Mercedes then told Kimberly about the cloud and email. Although Reggie seemed to think her investigation worthy, Mercedes felt less confident. To her surprise, her friend brimmed with excitement.

"This could be a great story! What if it is a new cloud or phenomenon? They might name something after you!" Kimberly gushed.

Mercedes laughed at her friend and felt better as she hung up. With a new burst of assurance, she ate a quick brunch and hit the road.

In preparation for her road trip, Mercedes downloaded a suspense novel and some podcast shows. She preferred to drive during the day because there was less chance of hitting a deer or a hog. This was Arkansas, after all.

The beautiful scenery of pine and oak trees with sun-glinted leaves relaxed Mercedes as she drove. She turned on the audiobook, but instead of focusing on the narrator reading the chapters of the story, her mind kept drifting back to past chapters of her own life.

In high school, she started dating the youth pastor's son. She had totally fallen for him even though her mother told her to slow down. Mercedes rolled her eyes as she remembered how at seventeen, she had her life all planned out with Garret King. He had irresistible charm, which resulted in her first kiss. Well, the first of a lot of things—things that for sure would have made his mother smack him on the back of his head. Senior King served as the youth pastor at their church. Mercedes assumed Garret to have some sort of standards or boundaries. By their third date, she learned that he did not and was unprepared for how far he wanted to go physically. She loved him, though, and matched his passion. If they hadn't broken up, he probably would have persuaded her to have sex. His father discouraged Garret to continue dating her. Mercedes believed Sr. King thought her unworthy of his son, who seemed destined for ministry and great things. They dated seriously for several months until Garret broke up with her. Mercedes had been devastated. She felt so worthless that she couldn't see what was genuine anymore. She felt uncomfortable going to the youth group because Garret and his dad were there; instead, Mercedes would sit with her parents and wait for Sunday school to be over.

Her only solace was the role she served in the music ministry. Mercedes had played the piano for a few church services. Then the church hired a new song leader, whose wife also played the piano. After a few snide comments from both of them that left Mercedes feeling her talent inadequate for service, she stepped aside and relinquished that ministry. *How could they have said such hurtful things to me, a teenager and somewhat new Christian? How could so-called Christians be so cruel?*

A few months later, she escaped to college, where she buried herself in coursework. Her college roomie, a Christian, would drag her to church events and singles' activities. When Mercedes finally started trusting people at her roomie's church and decided to get involved, she graduated and began her career.

Looking back at her years as a youth made Mercedes cringe. How could she have been so naïve and stupid? And where was God in all of this? *He stopped you from going too far with Garret. He gave you a Christian roommate to help ease your pain.* The two thoughts burst through her questions of doubt and echoed loudly in her mind.

A horn suddenly blasted from behind Mercedes as a trucker streaked past her. Mercedes struggled to keep her anger under control. "I hope you get a speeding ticket," Mercedes muttered under her breath. Cops often set up speed traps on that road, and she knew better than to speed.

Mercedes could never get away with anything. She tried to sneak out of the house once and got caught by her dad. Twice she was running late and decided to test the speed limit. She got pulled over and received a ticket each time. Once in college, the girls were talking about their dorm mom. As soon as Mercedes began to speak, the lady appeared behind her. Mercedes apologized profusely, but the damage had been done.

Forty-five minutes later, driving up and down narrow winding roads and thanking the Lord she didn't get carsick, Mercedes finally reached the town. The Shady Springs B&B was on her right next to a park with a pond and a hardware store. Across the street from the B&B stood a donut shop and a washateria. Farther down the road was a doctor's clinic and a small, square brick building with a white sign that read, "City Hall."

After parking at the inn, Mercedes got out and stretched her legs. She gazed at the mackerel sky. Her grandmother had always referred to it as a buttermilk sky. *Some see fish scales, where others see clotted milk*, Mercedes mused. However you described it, those cirrocumulus clouds were often indicative of weather change. *A storm of change is coming.* For some reason, this thought left Mercedes unsettled. Mercedes wasn't sure if she could handle any more change. She shook her head at her nonsense. Arkansas weather changed all the time. She pulled her suitcase and pillow out of the trunk of her car and walked up the steps to the B&B.

Shady Springs Bed and Breakfast was a beautiful old Victorian house painted yellow with white trim and shutters. Mercedes opened the door, and a little bell sounded, signaling her arrival. She rolled her luggage across the thick, Persian rug to a cherry wood counter where a rosy, older woman greeted her.

"Mercedes, we are so thrilled to have you stay with us! To think, we have a real celebrity right here in Shady Springs. I'm Gertie. We spoke on the phone." Gertie paused long enough for Mercedes to quickly reply with a "thank you" before continuing. "I've put you in the blue room. It's our balcony room. I think you will enjoy the scenery and the clawfoot tub in the bathroom. We only have one other guest right now, so it's fairly quiet. Are you here for rest and relaxation or visiting family?" Gertie enquired.

"Actually, I heard about an unusual cloud that has been hovering around, and I came to see it for myself. Do you know anything about it?" Mercedes asked hesitantly. Kimberley's pep talk had faded, and she began to question her own sanity. *You're wasting your time on this wild goose chase.* But Gertie absolved her doubts as she handed her an old skeleton key.

"Here's the key to your room. You've come to the right place! That cloud is a town legend, and I've grown up here my whole life. I can tell you all about it. Why don't you take your things to your room and get settled in? When you're ready to talk, come back down. Your room is up the stairs, second room on the left."

Mercedes agreed as she took the ornate key. It felt heavy in her hand. She eyed it curiously.

"It's a skeleton key, an antique," Gertie explained. "I just love them—much more character than those cheap plastic cards the modern hotels use nowadays. Oh, we do have a resident cat, Mr. Jingles. You're not allergic, are you?" Gertie looked at her with worry.

"Not at all. I love cats," Mercedes assured her. She began to climb the dark wood staircase that was contrasted by pale, yellow walls and framed by an ornate archway. The stairs curved round into a hallway. The walls on the second floor were painted with light grey and white vertical stripes with a dark wood trim.

Mercedes unlocked her door and entered her room by turning the vintage glass doorknob. She didn't really have much experience with B&Bs, so she wasn't quite sure what to expect. When she thought of B&Bs, she thought of antiques, floral wallpaper, and outdated furniture. Her room, however, had been updated. Appropriately sanctioned "the blue room," the bedroom consisted of a king-sized brass bed with a pale blue, quilted top and an assortment of blue and white pillows. Photos of the house pet adorned the room's white walls. The photographs had been printed with a blue filter that looked cute and modern in their black picture frames. Blue curtains framed the French doors that led to a small balcony. Through the doors, Mercedes could see the pond.

Mercedes laid her suitcase on the chaise lounge positioned in front of the doors, put her things away, and used the restroom. Relief flooded over her when she saw that the bathroom had been updated as well with white subway tiles and new sink fixtures. The clawfoot tub was in pristine condition, and plush white towels were folded neatly on a shelf. Mercedes snapped a few pictures of her room and sent them to her Mom with a text letting her know she was okay.

When Mercedes returned downstairs, Gertie waited with another elderly lady. They were both sitting in the parlor room, adjacent to the check-in room. Gertie asked Mercedes if she would like some hot tea, which Mercedes graciously accepted.

The other lady began to pour as Gertie introduced her. "This is my younger sister, Bertie. She helps me run the inn," Gertie explained. Bertie sat upright, tall and thin in contrast to her sister.

Mercedes replied, "Nice to meet you."

"I absolutely love it when you do the weather on TV," Bertie said, handing her a gold-rimmed floral teacup. "You're my favorite to watch."

"Wow, thank you." Mercedes took a sip. "I guess I should tell you both that I'm no longer with the news station. They had some cutbacks, and, well, I didn't make the cut."

Bertie put her cup down. "Oh, I am so sorry to hear that! I sure hope that Tucker something or another isn't still on. I don't trust anything he says. He comes across like an oily car salesman."

Mercedes tried not to smile and shrugged her shoulders. "I'm not certain who the station will be deciding on." She tried to steer the conversation back to the cloud. "So, what can you tell me about this town legend?"

Gertie answered her. "It all started back when the town was founded by Judd Hart, Shady Spring's pastor. He believed that God led him and his family to settle the town here. He had a wife and two children. Later on, his wife was murdered—that's a tragic story. Anyhow, his family has all passed now, but the story carried on through generations about Pastor Judd following a cloud to this area."

"So, he thought he was being led like Moses? Like with the children of Israel? Forgive me. This is a little out there for me." Mercedes wrinkled her nose.

Gertie took a sip of her tea. "Throughout history, people have asked God for a sign or miracle, some sort of confirmation of the path they were supposed to take or help out of a situation. That doesn't necessarily make you crazy. Sometimes a wisp of faith is all we have to hold on to. The difference is who we place our faith in. Pastor Judd's situation was probably pretty desperate. Arkansas in the 1850s wouldn't have been easy to travel through."

Bertie's hands began to tremble as she set her teacup down, spilling the amber liquid on the lace tablecloth. "Some people say that the cloud remains above the lake as a testament of the town's faith. That's what has gotten some people all worked up. It seems as if the cloud is getting smaller every day. Is this because God is displeased with our town? Have we wronged Him in some way?" Bertie's voice escalated.

Mercedes could see this was upsetting to her. She tried to divert the issue by addressing Gertie. "Well, I would love to go see this cloud for myself. Could you give me directions where to best observe it?" asked Mercedes.

"Of course, I'll draw you a little map. It's not very far from here." Gertie motioned for Mercedes to follow her back to the check-in counter.

Mercedes got up and turned to say goodbye to Bertie, but Bertie wiped the spots on the tablecloth and mumbled to herself, almost as if she was in another world.

"I'm so sorry about that. Bertie has good days most of the time, and she was so excited to meet you. She is in the middle stage of dementia."

"That's okay. I appreciate all of the information, and I'm sorry it upset her so."

"I don't need to draw you a map either," Gertie stammered. "It's simple to get there. Go right and then turn left on the street by City Hall. That road will veer right, and you just follow it till it dead-ends at Shady

Springs Lake. Our church and a few restaurants are on the lake too. It's about a ten-minute drive."

"That sounds easy enough."

"Also, we're having roast and potatoes for dinner. Dessert is bread pudding or chocolate cake. That is if we haven't scared you off."

"Dinner sounds wonderful," Mercedes reassured her and walked out the door.

As Mercedes started her car, she wondered about Bertie's reaction. The woman was visibly upset about the cloud diminishing. Did Bertie really believe the cloud correlated with God's approval or blessing? Could she herself believe that God led people here by a cloud? *Miracles happen every day. Am I not a God of miracles?* A voice gently reminded her. Then, she remembered a quote her professor always spouted from Albert Einstein: "There are only two ways to live your life. One is as though nothing is a miracle. The other is as though everything is a miracle."

Alright, fine. I do believe in miracles. Mercedes relented. *And it would be awesome to see a miracle—but there could also be some scientific rationale for this phenomenon. It's much too early to succumb to any theory yet,* Mercedes reminded herself. Cumulus clouds have a lifespan of less than an hour. Lenticular clouds, maybe a few hours. How could this cloud have existed all these years? Hope and curiosity drove her to the object of her interest.

2

GRANT

We just have to trust Him. In our waiting,
He is working.

—Harold

Grant Ford studied the two men who sat across from him in his office. Harold Martin and Chase Westin had served as deacons at Shady Springs Church since Grant had been just a boy. After Grant's father died while serving in the Army in the Afghanistan War, the men stepped in to help raise Grant and his sister, Alice.

Grant would never forget the day when Harold and Chase came knocking on their door. The bank had called about their past-due mortgage, and his mother was beside herself. Carol Ford had gone into her bedroom and shut the door. Grant could hear her voice carry over through the vent in his room. "Lord, I don't know how to do this. I don't know how to make this work. But you know how, God, and I know you can provide a way. Please don't let us lose our house. Please, God," his mother sobbed.

Moments later, the deacons from church arrived. They had been praying earlier in the week and decided the Lord wanted them to give the Ford family a love offering. They had a check for the exact amount of the past-due mortgage. It was a pivotal point in his mother's faith. She knew she could get through this situation, and she wasn't alone.

It was an amazing moment in Grant's faith—to actually see God answer a specific prayer like that. He had heard missionary stories about God meeting their needs, but to actually see it happen for himself felt incredible.

Harold and Chase were not your typical senior church members. They were a pastor's senior dream team, men of wisdom and character. Both were tough and hardworking and reminded Grant a little of John Wayne and Chuck Norris. Grant took their sage advice and suggestions seriously. As he observed their red-rimmed eyes and slumped shoulders, Grant worried that they might have too much on their plates. They both taught Sunday school classes, served as deacons, and even helped with Good News Bible Clubs in the Shady Springs School District. That morning, the men were having a pastor meeting before their usual monthly business meeting.

"Well, Sunday school classes seem to be holding steady, and the new young adult class seems to be taking off," Grant said as he handed them the following month's attendance sheets. There had been some discussion about getting rid of the Sunday school classes.

When Grant went to Bible college, he was astounded by how little his colleagues knew about simple Bible stories. He himself had learned so much doctrine and Bible truth just from attending Sunday school as a child. Grant felt people needed to know what they believe and why they believe it if they were going to make a stand in the world for Christ.

He still remembered his favorite Sunday school teacher, Mrs. Strickland. She smelled like JERGENS® lotion, and she would give him a trinket every Sunday morning when he could come in and recite his memory verse. Those verses remained in his heart.

Harold tapped the spreadsheet. "Our numbers appear healthy. I think the different ministry outreaches and activities have also helped with attendance."

When Grant took on the role of pastor at the church, the numbers were dwindling and had more activities geared toward their senior members. Grant kept the senior activities going but also instated the Bible Club ministry in the schools and other family outreach activities.

Chase piped in. "Pastor Grant, the way the church is starting to grow again is exciting. I can assure you when we start growing, the devil starts fighting, and that's what has started to happen now."

Grant had thought things were going really well. "What do you mean? I haven't heard any mention of discontentment."

"It's the cloud," they answered simultaneously. Harold added, "It's shrinking."

Grant didn't understand what they were getting at. "I know what the cloud represents to our town history, but I'm not sure I understand how this relates to our church." Folklore circulated from before his time that the town was founded by a preacher who followed the cloud to its current location. He led his congregation through the Arkansas wilderness like Moses led the children of Israel around Mount Sinai. There was no documentation to prove the claims; only tales passed down for generations.

"Some people in our town perceive the cloud as a reflection of the church," Chase explained. "Others perceive the cloud as a reflection of the pastor."

Grant rubbed his beard thoughtfully. "So, people really think the cloud diminishing is my fault? That correlates with my relationship with God?"

"I know it sounds crazy, but this whole town has always looked to the cloud as confirmation or approval from God," said Harold.

"And what do you make of the cloud?" asked Grant.

"I think the stories of the pastor and cloud are true. I've never understood why the cloud remained. Has it been God reminding us of what He has done for us? Is it a reminder of his faithfulness? I can't say for sure," answered Harold.

"What we do know for sure is you, Pastor Grant." Chase stared him in the eye. "Our church is where it is today because you have been seeking God's will for our congregation. Harold and I and the more active members have seen it firsthand."

"Unfortunately, some of the old family lines in our church have more faith in that cloud than they actually do in God. These families and some of the councilmen have real power in our church," Harold interjected.

Grant knew what the men meant when they said the families had power. A few of the deacons and councilmen ruled the town and had run off the last pastor. The poor fellow had wanted to exchange the pews for chairs and bring in a keyboard. Grant had been pastoring Shady Springs for three years and managed to avoid any conflict with them—until now. "Are they talking about removing me?" He felt like he'd been punched in the gut. He had given everything he had to minister to the people of Shady Springs. Heck, most of them he had known his whole life.

Harold leaned back and crossed his arms. "They're a bunch of idiots if they do. They have no ground whatsoever."

Chase shook his head. "We've only heard some grumbling from those who work around them. The councilmen will ask to meet with us before meeting with you. You can be sure we will go to bat for you."

This was totally over Grant's head and out of his hands. He had no control over that cloud. This being his first pastorate, he lacked experience in dealing with these kinds of matters. He ran his fingers through his light brown hair. "Thank you for letting me know what's going on and for standing behind me. It's disheartening, I'll admit, that they're so quick to dismiss me after three years as their pastor. Nonetheless, we know God is in control of the cloud and the hearts of the people."

"That's right," agreed Harold. "This thing is far from over. The Lord is doing something here. We just have to trust Him. In our waiting, He is working."

The three men ended their meeting with prayer, and Grant walked Chase and Harold out. When he returned to his office, he sat at his desk, mulling things over. He knew God was using him to revive Shady

Springs. His people were excited and were growing spiritually. They were eager to help in different ministries. *I know there were recent times in our church where the leadership and members were stagnant. Why is this happening now? And why to me? Is it Satan trying to undo my work and ministry?*

Grant began to de-clutter his desk as he reflected on his meeting with Harold and Chase. He placed his sermon notes in a stack and noticed one had fallen under his desk. The black walnut, kneehole desk was as old as the church. The town presented the beautiful antique as a gift to the founding pastor, Judd Hart. He reached underneath the desk to pick up his notes. "Ow!" Grant rubbed the already growing knot on the top of his head. He grabbed his phone and used the light from it to get a better view of what he had hit. A small knob protruded from underneath the top drawer. "Oh, cool!" Grant said to himself. The drawer had a false bottom; one had to be underneath the desk to see it and open it. Grant crawled underneath and carefully pulled the knob. A leather-bound journal with the letters J.H. imprinted on the front slid out into his hand.

He crawled back out and gingerly laid the journal on top of his desk. Everyone in town knew that Judd Hart founded the town back in 1850. The journal Grant found could've belonged to him. Grant carefully unwrapped the leather cord around the worn, tan cover and opened the book. On the first yellowed page, the words "Diary of Judd Hart" were written in script. Intrigued, Grant turned to the next page. His office phone rang, causing him to jump. He carefully closed the book and picked up the phone. "Pastor

Grant, it's Ryan. It's time, Pastor! Marie is having the baby! Can you come up to the hospital?" His panicked parishioner paused for air.

"Ryan, just breathe! Marie needs you conscious, alright? I'm on my way, brother. You're going to do fine!" Grant slid the journal into his desk and grabbed the keys to his Harley®. He received lots of feedback from the elders about his irregular ride. He refused to give it up.

The motorcycle was the one tangible object left that connected him to his dad. Everything else had been sold to help pay the bills. His dad had won the bike out of some crazy bet from an old Army buddy. Saturday mornings became a special routine for just the two of them working side by side. His dad would ask for a tool or part, and Grant would usually bring him the wrong one. While they worked, they would dream about all the places they would ride. After his father died, Grant had no idea how to continue working on the bike. He'd just sit and stare at the bike, crying. In the end, Harold helped Grant get the Harley running. One evening, Grant's mother called Harold over to get Grant under control. He'd been going through a rebellious stage and was acting out. The final straw was when his mother refused to let him go to a friend's house. He could feel the veins throbbing in his neck as he grabbed one of his mother's finer dinner plates and shattered it across the kitchen floor. "I hate you!" he screamed as he ran into the hot garage to seethe. When Harold entered the garage, Grant gave him his best death stare daring him to speak. To Grant's surprise, Harold didn't say anything, just stood and took a look around.

Harold walked over to the bike and patted the seat. "I remember your father working on this Sportster. He was so excited about getting it running."

Grant scowled. "Yeah, well, it will never start now."

Harold ignored Grant's disposition and did a quick inspection of the bike. "Keys?" he asked.

Grant rolled his eyes as he huffed past Harold and grabbed the keys from the pegboard wall. "Here."

Harold started the engine to only have it sputter and die.

Grant smirked. "Told you."

Harold went over to his dad's toolbox and pulled out some tools.

"Hey, what are you . . . those are my dad's!"

Harold paused. "You want to fix the bike, or what?"

Grant stood with his mouth agape as Harold handed him a wrench.

He stammered. "My dad loved this bike. We were supposed to fix it together and go on a road trip. We were going to go to the Little Grand Canyon."

The next hour, they worked side by side on the bike, and Grant felt his anger melt away. Harold showed him everything from the shifter drum to the clutch basket. He was totally in the zone and focused on the work. When his mom came in to check on them, Grant remembered his previous offences.

He could barely look at his mom when he apologized later that night. He vowed to never hurt or scare her like that again. Something changed in him that day, like a switch that softened his heart. Now, Grant recognized that touch as the Holy Spirit. While he didn't ride the motorcycle everywhere, he knew it would forever be a cherished possession. *Nope, I will never get rid of my Harley,* he thought. He also owned a little pickup truck he drove to church on Sundays and Wednesday nights. *Perhaps, if I ever get married and need more seats, I might trade in my truck—nah.* He dismissed that idea as well.

3

MERCEDES

Something about nature calmed her soul.

—Mercedes

When Mercedes' alarm went off at seven, she threw off her covers, eager to start her day. Rubbing the rising goosebumps on her arms, she stepped out on the balcony and watched the ducks lazily swim around the pond. It was a peaceful scene. Something about nature calmed her soul. Mercedes closed her eyes and breathed deeply. Another gust of brisk breeze jump-started her into getting ready, and she stepped back inside to get dressed. She had set out a navy top and white flowing cotton skirt the night before. She slipped on her Sperrys and a blue jean jacket, grabbed her purse, and fervently prayed for a coffee in her near future.

As she locked her room, she recalled the previous day's events. The cloud hovered over the lake, as Gertie had said. Its shape reminded Mercedes of an egg cooked sunny side up, suspended in air, with the lake serving as the saucepan. The thought of eggs began to make her stomach growl. Mercedes hoped that breakfast would be as stellar as dinner the night before. She could probably eat Bertie's delectable bread pudding for breakfast, lunch, and dinner.

Bertie had been in a much better frame of mind that evening, and Mercedes made sure to avert all cloud conversation from the table. Gertie played the perfect hostess but seemed slightly stressed. There had been some sort of mishap in the kitchen earlier. Mercedes also met the other guest at the hotel, an older gentleman named Hap Wharland. Hap wanted to relocate to Shady Springs and was lodging at the B&B till he could find a permanent residence.

As Mercedes entered the dining room, the smells of coffee and bacon permeated through the air. A nice spread of warmed bread pudding, bacon, eggs, and fresh fruit sat out on the credenza. Mercedes happily filled her plate. The two sisters sat at the table, reading the paper. They looked up and greeted her as she sat to eat with them.

"Good morning, dear! How did you sleep?" Bertie said as she laid her paper down.

"Wonderful," Mercedes said without hesitation. When she lay down last night, her body seemed to meld into the mattress. It was as if her body had said enough to the worries and anxieties weighing her down and switched to automatic shutdown.

"Fabulous," Bertie said. "What are your plans today?"

Mercedes paused and spoke before taking a quick bite. "I thought I would check out the newspaper archives in your library. I noticed it by the lake yesterday."

Gertie said, "I think it opens at nine. Our librarian is Mr. Wilcott. Don't be put off by his petulance; he's all bark and no bite."

Mercedes laughed. "Okay, is there anything else I should know?"

Gertie and Bertie looked at each other knowingly and replied in unison, "Pastor Grant!"

"Beg your pardon?" Mercedes questioned warily. She didn't like the secret smile the two women shared. She also didn't feel comfortable talking to a strange pastor.

Gertie's eyes widened. "He is our local pastor here, and the church building is a historical landmark. The original families have kept it really nice through the years."

Bertie continued, "You'll probably get some good historical facts from the minutes from the church books. Also, Pastor Grant is such a nice, caring young man."

Gertie insisted, "If you have time, you should stop by. It could give you valuable insight on the founding pastor and his family."

Mercedes threw her hands in the air in surrender. "Alright, I will go by after the library. I will probably grab some lunch on the lake while I am out there."

The two older ladies smiled happily while Mercedes sighed and ate her breakfast.

The rest of the conversation carried on about current events in the town, then to Mercedes' family. She told them about her parents and growing up in

El Dorado. Her mother had been a teacher and her father a pilot. Her dad served in the Air Force and now flew for private clients at their local airport. All in all, she had a pretty blessed upbringing. Mercedes hadn't really contemplated her childhood much, but she knew that just the fact that her parents were still happily married today put her in the minority.

At nine o'clock, Mercedes bid the sisters farewell and set out for the library. The daylight gave her a better view of the lake. The town expanded around the lake, making it the town's epicenter. Old buildings mixed in with the newer, creating a mishmash of architecture. An updated doctor's office stood next to the library, a tall, antiquated, red brick building. The boards creaked as Mercedes stepped under the library's white stoop and columns. She turned the knob and pushed open the red door.

In the center of the room, a gray-haired man sat behind a tall counter, reading a newspaper. There were aisles of books on all sides of the room labeled by genre. Two computers sat on a table against the wall. As Mercedes approached the counter, the man didn't stop his reading to acknowledge her presence.

"Excuse me," she said with a friendly smile.

"Hmm?" the man growled in response without even looking up.

The smile never left her face. "Are you Mr. Wilcott? Gertie said you were the most knowledgeable about Shady Springs history." Okay, she may have exaggerated a little bit, but as they say, you catch more bees with honey or, in this case, grumpy old men.

The man studied her with skepticism. "Is that so?"

Or maybe not. She tried again. "Do you have any books on the town's history or old newspaper clippings? I am trying to find out more about the town's founder and the cloud."

He cleared his throat and said slowly, "Is Bertie still making that bread pudding up there?"

Mercedes politely affirmed that the bread pudding was delicious, then silently counted to ten so she wouldn't strangle the man.

"Well, our town papers are all on microfilm. Are you familiar with using them?" Mr. Wilcott sighed at the inconvenience.

"Actually, I am. We used them for research in college." Mercedes tried to keep a pleasant expression on her face.

Mr. Wilcott harrumphed and crossed his arms. "Alright then. Let me show you where everything is."

He led her through a door on the back wall that opened to a small room that held the microfilm reader and metal file cabinets with the microfilm inside. "If you are searching for information on the founding pastor, Judd Hart, these films contain early newspapers from the neighboring town, Cedar Ridge. Their town was founded before Shady Springs and began running its editions in 1845. Shady Springs was established in 1850, and we began running our own newspaper in 1855." He selected a few white boxes labeled by newspaper name and the circulation date.

"Thanks," Mercedes said as she sat down at the table. She pulled out the tray on the microfilm projector and began to load the Cedar Ridge film from 1850 onto the rollers while Wilcott scrutinized her every move. After a few awkward moments, he seemed satisfied with her competence and ambled back to the front desk. Mercedes let out an exasperated sigh of relief when he left.

The cholera epidemic that ravaged the nation during the mid-nineteenth century almost decimated Cedar Ridge. Mercedes scanned countless articles about cholera deaths. One account reported up to thirty lives claimed in a twenty-four-hour period from the dreaded disease. The article print was tiny and faded in some areas. As she searched, she kept finding herself sidetracked by funny nuances relative to the period like "consummate humbuggery."

Finally, Mercedes found an article that recounted the founding of a new city—Shady Springs. The paper reported Reverend Judd Hart had founded the town with his wife and two children. He and ten other families of his congregation had moved to the area after cholera rampaged through the last small community they had tried to build. They christened the town "Shady Springs" because of the temperate climate around the lake. Mercedes pursed her lips. The article didn't give a lot of information—no mention of the cloud at all or the pastor's so-called journey of faith.

Mercedes put in the Shady Springs's newspaper film of 1855. Again, no mention of the cloud. There were weekly articles by Reverend Judd, items available at a general store, obituaries and weddings, and articles from bigger newspapers like the *Washington Telegraph* and the *Weekly Arkansas Gazette*. In 1856, Mercedes paused to read an article on the death of Reverend Judd's wife, Glennis.

Mrs. Glennis, our town mother, was tragically shot late last evening. Reverend Hart has requested the details of this horrific event be omitted from our periodical. Says the reverend, "A terrible accident has occurred, and our hearts are filled with anguish. There is no guilty party here." Sheriff Harper has also commented that "there is no evidence of foul play, only an unfortunate event of affliction."

Mercedes scanned the article for further information, but it only contained Glennis Hart's obituary. She wondered what misfortune fell upon the poor woman and why they had left it out of the paper. Whatever the mysterious reason, it didn't have anything to do with the cloud. Mercedes rubbed her eyes and looked away from the screen.

The door to the room opened, and Mr. Wilcott came in. "Well, how goes it? Have you found what you were looking for?"

Mercedes slumped in her chair. "No, not really. To be honest, I'm not really sure if I am going to find anything useful."

Mr. Wilcott tapped the gray whiskers on his chin. "It seems I remember there being some articles written about our town founder for the Shady Springs centennial celebration. That would have taken place in May of 1955. Would you like to take a gander at those?"

Mercedes straightened her shoulders. "Sure," she replied. "Thank you, Mr. Wilcott."

He handed her the film and said gruffly, "You can call me Paul."

Taken back by the sudden camaraderie, she nodded her head and began putting the film in the machine.

She heard the door close behind her as she began to study the news columns. It was staggering to see the progress over a hundred years. These articles were filled with comics, movie advertisements, and photographs. Mercifully, the font appeared larger and easier to read. She paused and smiled as she read about a student who brought an alligator to school for show-and-tell. The alligator caused "quite a ruckus" when it bit the student's unfortunate teacher.

Aware of getting sidetracked again, Mercedes kept scanning till she found the article or rather articles she was seeking. The town had printed a special edition paper for the centennial celebration. A photograph of a sixty-year-old Reverend Hart with his adult children taken in 1895 displayed on the cover. Mercedes studied the photo, trying to get a feel of the man. A respectable picture at the time, when people preferred solemness instead of smiles. Judd Hart looked like the typical reverend, and Mercedes had to admit he had some handsome features. His children, on paper, portrayed reputable adults. As she studied their faces and body placement, Mercedes noticed they stood close to their father as if protecting him, and their chins were pointed up as if they were ready to challenge or defend.

Next, Mercedes read the articles written by the elders of the town. They all testified that Reverend Hart founded Shady Springs and claimed he and his congregation abandoned their previous homes due to the cholera epidemic. During the two-week journey, the Lord provided a cloud to shade them, and they followed the cloud to its resting place at Shady Springs. Not one townsman questioned the man's sanity or behavior. *I suppose this newspaper article adds to the validity of the town's claim. It's only one article, though; I need something more concrete.*

That reminded her she needed to research the weather history of the town and check for any change in weather patterns that could explain the cloud's demise. She spent another hour looking at the weather and climate data of the area but couldn't find any reasonable answer for what was happening.

After she emailed herself copies of the articles she might want to reread for later, Mercedes grabbed her purse and headed toward the door. She said thank you to Mr. Wilcott, or Paul, rather, and exited the library.

Mercedes basked in the warm sunlight and fresh air before deciding to walk over to the church. It was only four or five blocks from the library, and she needed the time to work up the nerve to speak to Pastor Grant. Mercedes didn't trust Bertie and Gertie's schoolgirl mannerisms. Picturing the man homely and studious, she trudged past a bait-and-tackle shop, a restaurant, and an ice cream shop before arriving at the church.

Shady Springs Church consisted of two buildings. The first was a picturesque white building with green shutters and a steeple with a bell tower. A historic landmark plaque proudly posted on the property. A newer building stood beside the chapel, probably the fellowship hall where the congregation could gather informally. Mercedes followed the sign that read "pastoral offices" leading to a side door.

Here goes nothing, she thought to herself. Taking a deep breath, she pushed open a glass door that opened into a small hallway. There was one door on the left and three on the right. She quickly deduced the first two doors on the right were restrooms, and the last one, with the door open, must be the pastor's office. Sure enough, a man poked his head out the doorway.

"Oh, hey!" he greeted her as he began to walk toward her. "I thought I heard the door open! My name is Grant Ford. How can I help you?"

Mercedes took a step back. She hated to describe a pastor this way, but well, Grant Ford was hot. Around her age, he stood about average height with a medium build, and his almond-colored hair tousled on top laid neat and trim around his ears. Bright, brown eyes smiled at her as he spoke to her.

"You're the pastor?" She eyed him suspiciously. *Quit making this weird. Try and act normal, Mercedes.* These emotions abruptly dropped on her made her extremely uncomfortable.

"Guilty as charged." Grant laughed.

Mercedes smiled back at him, trying desperately to appear at ease. "Hi, I'm Mercedes Lewis," she began awkwardly. "I am staying at the B&B. Gertie and Bertie thought you might be able to help me. You see, I'm researching the cloud over the lake. I'm a meteorologist."

"Well, if you are digging for scientific data, I'm not sure I am going to be of much use," Grant replied.

"Actually, I'm trying to find more historical background. I've heard about the claims that the founding pastor believed the cloud led him to this lake," Mercedes explained.

A big grin spread across Grant's face.

Mercedes felt her face flush. *Okay, girl. You've got to get it together. He probably has this whole town swooning,* she told herself.

"You're not going to believe this. I just found Pastor Hart's journal in a secret compartment of my desk yesterday. I haven't had a chance to read it yet because I got called away to help a friend. I was about to examine it when you walked in." He motioned for her to follow him into the little office.

"Are you serious?" Mercedes exclaimed as she entered his office. "I was hoping to find an actual account of what really happened. The timing is perfect."

Not much occupied the tiny room. A bookcase lined the back wall with an antique desk centered in front of it. Two burgundy office chairs sat in front of the desk. Mercedes sighed in relief as Grant left the office door open behind them. His office brought back painful memories of hurtful words she shared with her youth pastor. She tried to shake the recollection from her mind and focus on what Grant had told her.

"You said you found a secret compartment in your desk?" She eyed the desk curiously.

"Yeah, it's underneath the desk. Here, come around and check it out."

Mercedes bent to look under the desk and felt the little knob. "This is so cool!" she said excitedly. She turned her head back quickly and conked Grant right in the nose. "Oh, my gosh! I am so sorry!" Her face grew hot as she scrambled to her feet to see Grant holding his nose. "Are you bleeding?"

"No, no. I'm okay. It's my fault. I should have told you I was behind you." Grant removed his hands to reveal a swollen nose.

"I'm sorry, really. Is there anything I can do?"

Grant laughed. "No, I'm fine. I have a big nose anyways. Here, let me show you the journal." Grant handed her a small leather-bound book off his desk and sat in one of the adjacent chairs in front of the desk. "It's kind of small, and the writing is a little faded, but it seems to be in good condition," Grant explained as he indicated to the chair beside him. "We can take turns reading it if you like," he continued. "I'm eager to see for myself what Pastor Hart has written."

Mercedes slowly sat down in the chair and examined the journal. She thought maybe she could scan the pages with her phone, but the journal itself was fairly thick. Plus, she had no way of knowing which pages to scan since it had never been read before. It looked like they were doing this together. She handed it back to Grant. "Alright. You read first."

4

GRANT

The cloud beckons to our band from afar off. It is hard to tell through the trees, but it appears the cloud is hovering over the lake.

—Pastor Judd Hart

Grant couldn't believe his eyes when he saw Mercedes Lewis for the first time. Of course, he recognized her from her weather reports on television. Trying to play it cool, he didn't mention he recognized her as a TV personality. *She probably has guys falling all over her*, he reasoned. With her dark blonde hair and sparkling hazel eyes, she was a knockout.

Mercedes seemed nervous entering his office, so he kept talking, trying to put her at ease. Grant didn't know if it was him or perhaps being in a church that was off-putting to her. He didn't recall any information about her religious background. Grant knew from his few years as a minister that outsiders had a lot of mixed feelings about the church in general. However, he also knew the Holy Spirit cut through those bindings and softened hearts. *God give me the words to say that will help Mercedes to be receptive to you.*

Clearing his throat and rubbing his still sore nose, Grant began to read.

Tuesday, June 4, 1850

I cannot even begin to convey the travesties I have witnessed upon humankind at this time. The cholera epidemic has ravaged through our small town of Haven. Everyone is quarantined in their homes except for the doctor, the coffin maker, and, of course, myself. Yesterday, I made calls to five families who lost their loved ones to this deadly disease. Their skin had turned bluish-gray and had shriveled with dehydration. In two cases, the people were contorted so that their hips were out of place and legs turned out so unnaturally the doctor had to force the hips back to get the body into the coffin. I recently received a letter from my cousin in Indiana, who decided to abandon his home after all four of the doctors had succumbed to the disasterly plague.

After much prayer, I have decided to gather my family and leave this place. I told my congregation tonight that we will leave at first light. Several members asked if they could accompany us on our exodus, and of course, I readily agreed. Selfishly, I wish I could take my precious family and leave tonight— away from everyone, away from the unseen enemy. If only I could cast off my responsibilities of caring for my flock, but alas, I am their shepherd, and I must heed to my Shepherd's call.

Glennis is busy packing everyone's belongings, and I can see the fear in her eyes. I've seen her break down and her shoulders quake when she's turned around and thinks no one is watching. My eight-year-old daughter, Mary, understands the reasons why we are leaving. She had several school friends who were claimed by the virus. Edwin, who is only five years old, views our move as one step closer to his dream of gold mining in California. We've worked so hard to build this home for us and our children. We've sweat blood and tears into this town.

A few of my congregation members challenged my decision as if I didn't have strong enough faith to stay and fight this invisible enemy. However, this plague shows no prejudice—man, woman, child, colored, religious or non—it will take all within its grasp. I refuted to my doubters that leaving the areas cholera had tainted was the sensible thing to do. My ministry was to the living, not to the dead. The death toll now outnumbers the living. So, in the morning, we will pack up our wagon and leave at morning's light. I don't know how many will make the sojourn with us, and I'm not sure exactly where we will be going. I know there is a lake to the west of us and a larger town north of there. The great unknown is how far the arms of this insatiable illness has reached.

Thursday, June 6, 1850

We are on the second day of this journey, and already, I am weary. When we met with those who decided to embark with us, I was unprepared for the number of families who wanted to leave. I had thought two or three families would join us. News spread to other citizens of our community who were not members of our congregation, and now, we have ten families in our wagon band.

The weather is hot and humid with no relief in sight. We began our journey with prayer, and each man prayed for our group's safety and health. We also prayed for God's Divine guidance along the way. Our group travels all day and camps at night. Earl and Anna Winter, an elderly couple, had the misfortune of their wagon wheel breaking, and we had to stop and help repair their wheel. It took most of the day to fix it, so we have not sojourned far.

I had the privilege of knowing Earl and Anna since I came to Haven eight years ago, and they have been like grandparents to my children. Earl says this trip is their last great adventure. I've never known such sweet or compassionate spirits. Lois Rosteller began to complain as soon as we came to a halt. He came to me in disbelief that the elderly should even be on this journey. Lois said that they would slow us down, and he had the audacity to suggest that we leave them. How could we leave them in the middle of nowhere? This man has little conscience, and I worry about his influence on the rest of our little tribe. He sneered as another man and I began to do the repair and then sauntered off to nap in his wagon. His wife, Sarah, seemed embarrassed at his behavior and hid behind their wagon, although she let her daughter, Emily, play with our Mary.

The Rostellers moved to Haven a year ago. Although Sarah and Emily had visited our church several times, Lois never graced a pew. I know many men like him, hardened from life and cynical. I also know that God can break through those walls, but it sometimes takes something akin to a cannonball to get through that exterior. I will have to keep my eye on him and offer many prayers for him.

I have to confess something bizarre and wonderful. The weather has been insufferably hot and humid for June. Whilst we were making repairs on the wagon wheel, a cloud hovered over our little gathering. Mary noticed the cloud at first.

"Look, father," she said excitedly, pointing up in the air. "God has provided us some shade for our journey!"

I paused for a moment, wiped the droplets of sweat off my brow, and looked up. "Indeed, He has! Thank you, Lord, for your goodness to us!" I motioned with arms outstretched to the sky and smiled at my daughter.

Her big blue eyes sparkled enthusiastically, and she ran off to join her friend Emily again. My son,

Edwin, our wild west cowboy, has been capturing the girls as Indian princesses, trying to coerce them to lead him to a treasure. Unfortunately, the clever princesses keep escaping his snares. Oh, to be young and carefree again!

The children's escapades provide us some much-needed entertainment and laughter. The same cloud hovered over us during our labor, and when we were packed up ready to go, it seemed to float in the direction that we were heading. Then again, when we paused for the evening to set up camp, it seemingly stayed with us! I am grateful for the shade it provided and the comfort it gave to my people, if only but a day.

Grant stopped reading. Mercedes perched on her seat, hanging on to every word. "Do you want to read now? It looks as if the next few entries have to deal with the cloud."

Mercedes smiled gratefully and carefully took the ivory pages. She began to read while Grant listened on.

Saturday, June 8, 1850

We are on day four now. Our movement has been slow and steady. We rise early and have breakfast, typically bacon, bread, and coffee. The young ones have milk thanks to our dairy cows. Every family has brought their livestock, so we travel with the sounds and smells of cows and goats and chickens.

Samson, our ox, christened by Edwin, leads our wagon. Glennis gives me a break driving in the morning and afternoon. My backside is so sore from the jostling of the wagon the springs under my seat provide little comfort. The ride is unbearable for other passengers, so the children and Glennis walk alongside, helping control our livestock.

We stopped at noon and had some grits and apples for lunch. We passed the Southwest Trail today and saw travelers heading north toward the Arkansas River. Edwin counted fifteen wagons in their party. They were several yards away from us, so we didn't get to question their whereabouts or destination. We all had to listen to Lois Rosteller's ruminations of leaving us and joining their group. Lois felt sure that their party would be much livelier than ours. They were most likely going to a big city, which would mean less work than starting completely over, he reasoned. I reminded him of the cholera epidemic ravaging the larger cities and how God had been providing for us and protecting us on our journey.

I must confess I am most concerned about the disease pursuing us and having to handle death along this way. Praise the Lord that everyone seems to be in good health. This brings me to my most interesting news. Mary's cloud has stayed with us for three days now. We've grown accustomed to referring to it as Mary's cloud since it was she who first discovered it. Mary says the cloud reminds her of her mommy's hotcakes. It's a rather unusual shape for a cloud, like a rounded pillar.

I am wrestling with the decision of which way to head tomorrow. If we head north of the lake, we will reach Cedar Ridge, a town already established with easy access to supplies and goods. I have this strange heaviness in my heart that we will be met with great devastation if we take residence there. I cannot explain it; it is not fear, more like intuition. I plan to speak to Glennis tonight to see where her heart lies. Most of my congregation will follow where I lead them. Lois Rosteller, I know, will challenge me. He has already expressed an eagerness to reach Cedar Ridge. Another young fellow, Samuel Green, has gravitated to Lois, and I worry about his influence on Samuel as well.

Sunday, June 9, 1850

After breakfast today, we had a prayer meeting and a service. I preached on God's faithfulness to the children of Israel while they were in the wilderness and read 1 Corinthians 10. It seemed to encourage our little band. Anna taught the children to sing "Fairest Lord Jesus." The sweet, innocent voices filled the woods around us with such a cheer that even Lois Rosteller looked a little teary-eyed. When they sang "Ruler of All Nature," I couldn't help but think of our faithful cloud.

I feel we must stay united in this journey of faith. We have about two days sojourn left, and the excitement of new beginnings has begun to resonate in our hearts. Earl and Edwin did a little hunting and caught a couple of rabbits, which helped improve the camp spirit. The only dark cloud of the day was this evening when we discussed which way we should depart tomorrow. Lois has banded together with a few more men who wish to head for Cedar Ridge.

The unity we shared this morning seemed brief, and I fear we're divided again. I pray the Lord will grant me guidance as I lead us tomorrow.

Monday, June 10, 1850

I prayed for the Lord's guidance, and it seems as if He has given it. Mary's cloud drifted from us toward the direction I had been favoring, much to the dismay of Lois. We noticed it gravitating that way during breakfast, and Mary exclaimed, "Father, the cloud is leading us that way! Just like he led Moses and the children of Israel!" Lois snorted in disbelief, but I do believe this was the confirmation I needed on which way to embark. I told our group our destination while Lois shook his head in disagreement. We should have one more day of arduous travel, and then the real work will begin. I grow in confidence as the cloud stays with us on our journey.

Tuesday, June 11, 1850

Bereavement settled over our camp this morning. Earl's wife, Anna, passed away during the night. My heart aches for my friend. The loss of his wife, his life-long companion, is a devastation to the heart and soul I cannot even fathom. We are so close to our journey's end. Earl pleaded for us to wait to bury

Anna so she wouldn't be alone out in this wilderness, and thus, we obliged. Much to everyone's surprise, Lois collected spare wood and crafted a make-shift coffin. Every family donated some salt to help with her preservation.

As we began to travel our last day's journey, Lois told the group his family would not be traveling with us any farther. They would be heading for Cedar Ridge and welcomed anyone who would want to join them. Mary cried for days to be separated from her friend Emily, and I could tell that Glennis was saddened as well. Glennis had become quite close to Lois's wife, Sarah, over the last few days. The loss of her old friend and her new friend the same day has been a strain on her. Samuel Green left with Rosteller, but that was all who decided to dissent. The cloud beckons to our band from afar off. It is hard to tell through the trees, but it appears the cloud is hovering over the lake. We will survey the land at morning light.

As Mercedes finished reading, Grant's stomach rumbled loudly. "Sorry." Grant grabbed his belly, embarrassed. "I skipped breakfast this morning."

Mercedes laughed. "That's okay. I ate a huge breakfast and am pretty famished too. I guess it's lunchtime."

"Let me guess, bread pudding?" Grant replied with a grin.

"That bread pudding is sinful." Mercedes laughed.

"Do you want to go get something to eat? We can take a break and then come back and finish reading the journal?"

Mercedes hesitated, and Grant realized how much he wanted to get to know her better. "The diner is only a few blocks away, and they have amazing food—pie, burgers, salads."

Mercedes gave him a million-dollar smile. "Okay, you sold me. You had me at pie!"

5

MERCEDES

It is now more evident to me than ever that when God gives guidance, He also gives provision.

—Pastor Hart

In her angst about meeting Grant, Mercedes failed to notice the motorcycle parked outside the front of the church. "Is that your ride?" she asked incredulously.

Grant chuckled. "Yep, much to the dismay of some of our church elders. I usually drive my truck on days I have church service. You know, so my suit and tie don't get messed up. Do you ride?"

"No way! Those things scare me. My dad rides, though, and my mom sometimes will ride with him."

"What scares you most about motorcycles?"

The cool breeze from the morning departed, and Mercedes felt the humidity of the afternoon approach. She slipped her jacket off and wrapped it around her waist. "Losing control, I guess. As you, unfortunately, found out earlier when I conked your nose, I'm a tad bit accident-prone." This was an understatement. Mercedes had been banned from her local gym after her third mishap with the treadmill. The gym owner said she was too much of a liability. *No need to confess all my faults to the preacher man.* "I don't like skiing or bicycling, either, because I'm afraid I will go too fast and crash." She let out an embarrassed laugh. "There's probably some sort of psychopathy that goes with that."

"You don't seem like someone who would let fear stop you from a goal, though."

"True. If someone says I can't do something, then I usually have to prove them wrong."

Grant grinned at her. "Well, you never know. You might be a biker yet. Do you mind walking? I'll let you set the pace."

"Walking I can handle." Mercedes smiled and tried picturing herself on a motorcycle to no avail. An image of her on a bike with Grant—her arms wrapped around him—jolted her back to reality. *Best get those thoughts out of my head,* she chided herself. *He's a preacher and would never be interested in someone like me.* Mercedes turned the conversation back to him as they passed the ice cream shop. "How long have you been the pastor in Shady Springs?"

"About three years. Before that, I went to seminary in Texas. I felt God calling me into the ministry in high school. I grew up in Shady Springs, though, and always planned on coming back. How about you? Did you always plan on being a meteorologist?" he questioned.

So, he did recognize me after all. She couldn't help feeling a tiny bit pleased. "Yes, I've always had a fascination with clouds and science. They regulate the earth's temperature and impact the earth's climate. Then, there's simply the feeling of peace and encouragement you receive when you look at a sky filled with clouds." She sighed and kicked at a pebble with her shoe. "Anyways, weather became my passion and seemed like a natural field to go into after high school. I was a bit of a nerd. Still am, I guess." She smiled hesitantly at him and realized he was listening intently.

"Well, you're showing me clouds in a whole new light. I never really thought about their purpose up until now. It's amazing to me how intentional God was with His design. It seems everything He created provides a unique function."

Mercedes had never really given thought to clouds and science in relation to God and creation. *It is interesting how things in nature are intricately woven together.*

They reached the diner before they could discuss any further. A huge wooden sign read "Bluebonnets and Razorbacks" with a razorback painted with bluebonnets between its teeth. Mercedes looked at Grant in amusement.

Grant smiled as he opened the door and explained, "Roger and Darlene own the cafe. Darlene is a Texas girl, and Rog is Arkansan. Actually, he is a native of Shady Springs. The name is a compromise of sorts."

Mercedes followed Grant to a booth and sat across from him. A cheerful woman who looked to be in her thirties approached their table. Her name tag read "Darlene."

"Hey, y'all," she greeted them as she handed them a menu. "What would you like to drink?"

"I'll have an unsweet tea," Grant said.

Mercedes answered, "And I will have a sweet tea."

Darlene smiled at her and winked. "I knew you were a Southern girl."

"Pie and sweet tea? Someone has a sweet tooth," Grant teased.

Mercedes admitted, "I might have an itsy, bitsy problem with sugar, but let's get to the bigger issue here. What's good to eat?"

"The razorback burger is good, and so is the blue-bonnet salad. The key lime pie and the blackberry cobbler are also excellent," Grant advised.

Mercedes perused the menu and decided after her heavy breakfast she could use something on the lighter side. When Darlene brought their drinks to the table, Mercedes ordered the bluebonnet salad, and Grant decided to have one as well. As they sipped their drinks, Grant asked Mercedes about where she grew up.

"I grew up in El Dorado, south Arkansas," Mercedes explained. "It's a small town, although bigger than Shady Springs. And you pronounce it El Dorado with a long a—never pronounce it El Dorahdo. If you do, you will be marked an outsider for life."

"Duly noted," Grant said. "What about your family? Do they still live there?"

"Yes. My mom, dad, and granny still live in town. I'm also an only child, so I am used to getting my way."

Grant laughed. "I'll consider myself forewarned."

"I haven't been home in a while. I'm going there for a visit when I finish here."

"I bet your family will be excited to see you."

"My mom can't wait. Is your family from Shady Springs?"

"My mom still lives in town, and my sister is going to SAU in Magnolia, which I believe is close to your hometown," Grant replied as Darlene came up with their orders.

"Yes! Magnolia is not far from El Dorado at all."

"This looks great. Thanks," Mercedes told Darlene. The grilled chicken was cut diagonally atop bright, leafy greens with shredded cheese and tomatoes. There were also some freshly fried onions on the side with cayenne ranch dressing.

"Forgive me for being nosy, but I just gotta know! Are you Mercedes Lewis, the meteorologist?" Darlene asked.

Mercedes nodded her head in confirmation. "That would be me."

"Would you take a picture with me, please, so I could put it on our wall?" Darlene asked excitedly.

"Sure, we'll take one before we leave."

"Yay, thank you! Don't forget now," Darlene said as she rushed over to a table where four elderly women were gathered.

Mercedes felt a little embarrassed by all the attention in front of Grant. She wondered what his impression was of her. *Does he think I relish being in the spotlight? I basically told him I'm spoiled. Why did I say that? This is why I don't date. Whoa, girl,* she stopped herself. *This is not a date.*

Grant dug into his salad, thankfully unaware of her inner turmoil.

Strange, he didn't mention his dad. Mercedes didn't want to come right out and ask him about his father if it was a trigger subject. She tried to continue the conversation. "So, is your mom a part of your congregation?"

Grant paused from eating. "She is." He shrugged his shoulders. "Some might think it's kind of weird being a pastor to your mom, but she has been nothing but supportive to me. My dad died in the Afghanistan War when I was young, and my mom had to raise Alice and me by herself."

"Wow," Mercedes said. "Your mom sounds amazing. I'm sorry about your dad."

"Thanks. I'm blessed to have some father figures in the church who kept me on the straight and narrow. Who knows where I'd be today without their influence?"

Mercedes smiled and took a bite of her salad so she wouldn't have to comment. *What would her life look like now if certain people in the church had been less critical and more encouraging?* she wondered to herself. Something within her stirred and whispered back: *True encouragement comes from the Lord. Sometimes we need criticism to help us grow.* "What do you think of Pastor Hart's journal?" Mercedes changed the subject.

"It's amazing. It seems like God provided that cloud to help guide Judd Hart in the way he should go."

Mercedes had to agree, as far-fetched as it seemed.

"Excuse me," an elderly lady stood at their table, stopping Mercedes mid-sentence. One of the four women at the other table, poised with arms crossed, glowered at them. Mercedes saw Gertie had now joined the other ladies and waved at her.

"How can I help you, Mrs. Gladys?" Grant asked, setting down his fork.

"Pastor Grant," Gladys spoke in a no-nonsense tone, "the women's society is most concerned with Shady Springs's cloud disintegrating. Are you aware that the cloud is shrinking at this very moment? What are you doing about it?"

Grant gave her a warm smile and answered calmly. "Yes, Gladys. I am very aware of the status of our cloud. However, you and I both know there is only One in control of all the weather and nature, and I am not He."

Well, Mercedes thought to herself, *he handled that pretty well.*

"Pastor Grant," Gladys repeated herself, undaunted by his passive answer, "some people believe that our cloud is in direct correlation to the faith of our town pastor. If that is true, perhaps you might proceed with more caution and chasteness!" She overemphasized chasteness and glared at Mercedes with distaste.

Mercedes felt her cheeks turn red hot and opened her mouth in protest. *This is why you don't do church,* a nasty voice whispered in her ear. *Already judging you, and they don't even know you.*

Before Mercedes or Grant could say anything, Gertie appeared behind Gladys and reprimanded her. "Gladys! You ought to be ashamed of yourself. Bothering Pastor Grant with business that he has no control over. You know his heart is for his congregation! And don't you recognize Mercedes Lewis from the weather team on the news? She is in our town investigating our little cloud, trying to help!"

An awkward pause filled the air while Gladys pursed her lips and looked embarrassed enough to cry. "I'm sorry, Pastor Grant. I know I'm way out of line. Ms. Lewis, I hope you can forgive an old biddy like me. I get worked up over things, and well, I really am sorry."

Grant stood up and gave the lady a hug. "It's okay, Mrs. Gladys. I know you mean well."

Mercedes nodded at the distraught woman that it was okay as Gertie led Gladys back to their table.

Grant ran his hand through his hair and smiled apologetically. "I am so sorry about that, Mercedes."

Mercedes shook her head with a little laugh. "It's okay. I'm sorry if I tarnished your reputation."

"Trust me; these folks have known me my whole life. They've seen me through my rebellious teen years and more or less know all my transgressions. Going on a lunch date with an illustrious reporter? If anything, you are probably boosting my street cred." Grant tried to assure her.

Does he think this is a date? Should she let him pay if he offers? What is going on? Mercedes froze like a deer in headlights.

"I didn't mean like a real date, you know. Just lunch." He backtracked and stammered.

Relief flooded over her as she tried not to smile. His unease made him even cuter.

At nearly the perfect time, Darlene came to Grant's rescue and asked if they would like to have dessert. Tempted by the offer, Mercedes chose to decline. She really wanted to get back to the journal and read the next entry. Much to Mercedes' relief, they skipped the lunch payment discussion. Grant received free meals as a benefit from being a clergy, and Darlene refused to take Mercedes' money.

"The picture is your payment, honey!" Darlene said as she handed Grant her phone to take their photograph.

Derek Rossi walked with impatient strides through the doors of Shady Springs Church. His wife kept harping at him to seek Pastor Grant's advice about their marriage. Because Derek knew his wife was way too good for him, he obliged her wishes. He didn't understand why they needed counseling; it wasn't like they were fighting or anything. Sonja wanted to start adding on to their family, which Derek was fine with; however, Sonja kept saying that she wanted their kids to have a strong Christian background. To Derek, that meant just going to church, but Sonja seemed to think it meant something more. Derek thought about his parents. For the short time his parents were married, they had never gone to counseling. Perhaps if they had, his mom wouldn't have skipped out on them. Nope, he would not be finding any helpful tips about marriage from his side of the family—except maybe what not to do.

What does Pastor Grant know about being married anyhow? The dude isn't even married. Derek didn't like to admit it, but as a boy, he idolized Grant. It seemed he had the perfect life—he had a great family and was well-liked by everyone. The whole town made a huge deal when Grant went off to Bible college, then came back to serve as pastor. Derek secretly wished he had whatever Grant had. Derek had trusted Christ as a kid, but he didn't understand what made Grant so passionate about doing things at church.

The good pastor's office sat empty when Derek entered. *Looks like I'm not going to get to ask him about it today. Probably playing a round of golf somewhere.*

Derek sighed and took a peek at Grant's desk. *Typical pastoral stuff here, I suppose, but what is this?* His eyes fell on an old journal lying open on the desk.

Derek glanced around and picked up the journal. *Hey, if it was private, Pastor Grant wouldn't have left it out on his desk. I'll just read a bit and wait.* He settled into one of the chairs and carefully opened the leather bindings.

Monday, June 24th, 1850

Our days have been consumed with building houses and our church building. Of course, our first action of business was laying to rest Earl's wife, Anna. She was such a sweet lady, a grandmother to our whole congregation. Mary and Edwin took her death especially hard. Earl has seemed to throw himself into the daily labor of the town's development, and I worry about him overexerting himself. He is tenacious in his efforts and works harder and longer than the younger men in our party. We still have one more house to finish and an infirmary to construct. A few more families trickled into our township with men ready to help build our town. The Lord has also sent us a doctor. It is now more evident to me than ever that when God gives guidance, He also gives provision.

Sarah and Emily Rosteller came riding into town today. It appears Lois is having a hard time finding work in Cedar Ridge, and there's an outbreak of cholera, but I suspect there is another reason why his wife and daughter fled to us. Hues of brown and blue colored Sarah's wrists. I cannot fathom the deepest, darkest place a man has to go to injure a woman. But, for whatever reason, they are here, and we will provide a safe retreat for them. Mary is glad to have her friend back.

Sunday, June 30th, 1850

I failed to mention in my previous entry that our cloud remains. As I sit in reflection now, I see the silhouette of it, obscuring a few of the hundreds of stars we see at night. A few new town members take notice of its wispy tendrils and, after hearing our narrative of arrival thereby, comment on the comfort of its presence. It reminds me of the journey God has brought us through to arrive in this place we are now. We were comfortable and safe in Haven, aside from the epidemic. However, our new home gives us new ministries to different people. I pray our location by the water will draw more people to our town, thus providing more opportunities for the gospel to be shared.

Lois Rosteller attended church today. He sat in the back, trying to get in good graces with Sarah. I preached on Colossians 3:8-16 about putting off our sinful nature like anger and wrath and exercising mercy and forgiveness on each other. Lois smirked through the entire message, and I realized that instead of him focusing on his anger and wrath, he was going to try and use my sermon to get Sarah to give him another chance. I struggled with myself being able to show mercy to Lois. I so want to throttle the man and pray that the Lord gives me His own abundant mercy in order for me to restrain myself. I felt proud of Sarah later because she confided to

Glennis that she told Lois she did forgive him, but he would have to attend more than one church service for her to trust him again.

Derek flipped toward the end of the journal, and what he read made his hands tremble. He slowly closed the journal and stared at it for a solid minute. *If my wife ever found out about this, our marriage would be over for sure*, he thought to himself. *No one can ever know.* Derek slipped the journal into his pocket and quickly left the church.

6

MERCEDES

I can't imagine going through this life without the One True Companion.

—Gertie

On the way back to church, Mercedes realized she had more in common with Grant Ford than she thought. They liked the same kind of awkward humor in TV shows, and they both shared a love for British comedies. A connoisseur of tea, Grant told her about a place where he ordered his loose-leaf tea. The only unforgivable thing about Grant Ford was his disdain for sugar.

"It will be the fall of the human race," he said half-jokingly. "Did you know studies have been done on products to find the 'sweet spot?' They want their consumers to become addicted to their product."

Mercedes crinkled her nose. "Don't tell me you're a conspiracy theorist. It's going to take more than that to make me give up the trifecta—cookies, cake, and cola."

"I'm telling you—"

She playfully walked ahead of him, covered her ears, and told him not to tell her anymore about it. "Don't say any more; ignorance can be blissful!"

"Okay, okay!" Grant hurried to catch up with her. "I won't say another word about it. Today."

They both laughed. *Wow, I'm kind of having a good time. Who knew that hanging with a preacher could be fun?*

"Hey, how did you hear about our cloud anyways?" Grant asked as they neared the church.

"I received a strange email about it. At first, I thought it was a prank until I pulled up the town on the weather map. I'll have to show you the email sometime. You might be able to decipher who it's from."

Grant opened the church door for her, and they headed toward his office. When they entered Grant's office, Mercedes sat while Grant stood and stared at his desk.

"Do you mind if I take a photo of the pages we just read?" Mercedes began to dig around in her purse for her phone.

"Well, that may prove difficult to do." Grant began opening the drawers to his desk in a panic.

Mercedes stopped and stared at him. "What do you mean?"

"The journal's gone. I can't believe this. I should have locked my office door. Why would somebody steal this from me? I don't understand." He shut the last drawer with frustration.

Mercedes rose to help search, but they couldn't find many hiding spots in the tiny office. "Should we call the police?" Mercedes asked.

Grant sighed. "Not yet. Let me do some calling around and see if anyone knows anything. Maybe someone borrowed it."

If someone borrowed it, they surely would have left a note. Mercedes felt a gnawing pit grow in her stomach. "Well, I guess you can give me a call if you find out what happened to the journal." She grabbed her purse and handed him one of her cards with her phone number on it.

"Absolutely! As soon as I find out what happened, I'll call you."

They started to walk out when Grant stopped and said, "Wait, let me check the front entrance and make sure it's locked."

They went through the door that led to the auditorium to the front of the church. As they passed the platform, Mercedes couldn't help but stare at the beautiful baby grand piano.

"Do you play?" Grant asked as he gestured to the piano.

"Yes. I used to play a little at my previous church."

Grant began to respond when a petite, Hispanic woman entered from the door they came through.

"Pastor Grant, have you seen my husband?" The woman interrupted with her hand on her hip. Mercedes assumed the woman must be one of Grant's parishioners.

"Not today, Sonja. Sorry."

She furrowed her eyes. "Derek promised me he would talk to you today."

"Let me check and see if I have any missed calls," Grant said as he pulled out his phone. "Nope, no calls from him. Maybe he will stop by later?"

Sonja nodded doubtfully. "If you see Derek, will you have him call me, please?"

"Sure will," Grant replied as she walked out the door.

Mercedes half-heard their conversation. The piano beckoned to her. She hadn't played in such a long time.

Grant must have noticed her fixation because he suggested, "If you want to play it a bit, I don't mind."

Mercedes stepped back shyly. "That's alright. I don't want to be a bother."

"I'm going to be in my office studying and making some calls. It's no bother." Grant moved over and opened the lid to the keys. "Go for it."

Mercedes bit her lip and walked over to the piano. She ran her hand over the smooth, shiny lid. "Okay, thanks. I'll try not to make too much of a racket."

Grant smiled and gestured to his office. "I'll be back here if you need me."

Mercedes sat and played a few scales, getting a feel for the weighty keys. For her, playing the piano was such a stress relief; she forgot how much she enjoyed it. An old red hymnal sat on the piano stand, and she opened it up. She smiled when it fell open to "Turn Your Eyes Upon Jesus," one of her favorites. She began to play the first few chords. With each gentle keystroke, she felt the Lord pressing the heavy keys of her own heart. Tears ran down her face and silently splashed on the keys. For so long, she had just felt empty. She knew she was a child of God, but she felt like God was done with her. Through high school, she continued reading her Bible and praying, but the emptiness remained. Mercedes kept going through the motions of living the Christian life until she finally gave up. She stopped looking to Jesus, stopped pleading with God, and stopped relying on anyone else.

Mercedes finished the song and wiped away her tears. She turned the page and began to play another hymn. The music swept her away. Time seemed to disappear as the music poured from her, releasing the pain and fear within her—pain from all the past hurts and fear of the unknown future. After several more songs, Mercedes finally stopped for a break.

"That was beautiful," a voice said from behind her.

Startled, Mercedes turned around to see Gertie sitting on the front pew. "I came in to see Pastor Grant," Gertie explained. "I didn't mean to intrude."

"Oh, that's okay. I saw the piano, and I just had to play it. It's been a while since I've played." Mercedes grabbed her purse by the piano and walked off the platform toward Gertie.

Gertie held a box of tissue in her lap and dabbed her eyes.

"Are you alright?" Mercedes asked with concern.

"It's funny how a simple melody can dig up old memories. That last song you were playing, 'In the Garden,' was my late husband's favorite."

Mercedes sat down next to her. The woman before her had stood up for her at the restaurant. She would make time to listen. "'In the Garden' is my dad's favorite too. Has your husband been gone long?"

"A few years now. People say that losing someone gets easier with time, but I disagree. I suppose it's easier in the sense that I'm not consumed with the grief all the time, but every holiday, every trial I have to bear without him is a constant reminder that he's gone."

"I'm sorry. I can't even imagine the pain of losing someone so close." She tried to imagine if her mother lost her father or vice versa and the heartache they would feel. It would be devastating.

"I'm blessed, though, Mercedes. I have a heavenly Father I can go to, and He truly does fill that emptiness of a lost loved one. I can't imagine going through this life without the One True Companion." Gertie pointed up as she emphasized her last statement.

Mercedes nodded mutely. She felt if she said anything else, she would start crying too.

Gertie patted Mercedes on her hands and stood. "I'm sure you have plenty to do besides listen to the ramblings of an old woman. Were you able to find out anything today?"

Mercedes nodded as she tried to find her voice. "Grant found a journal of Pastor Hart's, and we were able to read some from it. Unfortunately, when we came back from the diner, the journal disappeared. Grant is trying to figure out what happened to it."

"Oh, dear! Do you think someone stole it?"

"I'm not sure. Grant seemed to think that perhaps someone borrowed it."

Gertie frowned as they started walking out the side doors to the office when Grant met them in the hallway.

While Mercedes had been playing the piano, Grant finished his sermon for the next night. Wednesday night remained one of his favorite services. Grant knew his people were tired midweek, so he challenged himself to keep his sermon shorter and more encouraging. He wanted to relight their fire to finish out the week. This month, he was preaching a series on the wanderings of the children of Israel. In his notes, Grant wrote: *The children of Israel witnessed miracles upon miracles of God's goodness and grace, yet they still had periods of doubt. How quick they were to forget God's deliverance or provision and turn their praises into protesting.*

Grant's thoughts veered to Pastor Hart leading his people and the miracle of the cloud. *I can't believe that someone stole the journal right off my desk. I really am going to have to start locking my office door.*

When the piano playing stopped, Grant heard Mercedes talking to someone. It sounded like Gertie, which caused Grant to remember his lunch with Mercedes. While they were walking to the diner, Grant noticed her eyes changed color from green to brown as the sunlight hit them from different angles. She really was beautiful. More importantly, he enjoyed talking with her, and he thought she enjoyed talking with him as well. It surprised him when she said she once played piano at church. Obviously very talented, he wondered why she had stopped playing. *There's a story there; I wonder what it is.*

Grant headed to the auditorium to see what was going on. He picked up his step as he approached them. He took in their red eyes and solemn demeanor. *God, comfort whatever it is that is burdening them and give me the wisdom to help.* "I thought I heard voices out here!" Grant said.

"I came by to see you, but I had to stop and listen to Mercedes' beautiful playing."

Grant nodded in agreement. "It was very inspiring. I actually feel like I accomplished some work today."

"Thank you." Mercedes ducked her head. "I'd better get back to the inn and see what else I can find out about this cloud. Thanks for letting me play on the piano." She practically ran out the church door.

I didn't even ask her how long she would be in town or invite her to our services. Grant wanted to follow her; instead, he focused his attention on Gertie and invited her to come to his office.

As Gertie began to sit, her words tumbled out in obvious distress.

7

GRANT

Am I still called? Am I worthy of this calling?

—Grant

"Pastor Grant, I just don't know what to do anymore. Bertie's dementia is getting worse. I'm not sure I can care for her much longer. When she made her bread pudding yesterday, she accidentally started a fire on the stove. Last Saturday, she wasn't making any sense and grew so upset I thought she might hurt herself."

Grant's heart broke for Gertie. He knew how close she was to her sister. He thought about his sister and how devastated he would be if he had to make this kind of decision himself. "I'm so sorry, Gertie. Are you thinking about someone coming to stay with her or maybe the nursing home?"

At the mention of a nursing home, tears began to well up in her eyes. "I think I'm going to have to put her in the home, mainly for her safety."

Grant walked over beside her and handed her a tissue. "We have a good home in town," he assured her. "Bertie will be taken care of there, and it's not far away. You could visit her anytime you like."

Gertie nodded as she dabbed the tears from her eyes.

"You shouldn't feel guilty about this decision either. You have done all you can. When the time comes to move her, I want you to call me. I can help, and I know Brother Chase and Brother Harold will come to help as well. You aren't alone in this," Grant promised.

Gertie agreed she would call him, and Grant had a moment of prayer with her.

As Gertie stood up to leave, she asked about his lunch with Mercedes. Grant shook his head knowingly at her and said it was fine. The old ladies in his church had been trying to set him up ever since he took the pulpit. He'd met more than his fair share of nieces and daughters from his well-meaning silver-haired ladies. Grant appreciated their intent, but he had a hard time opening his heart to anyone. He had loved before and lost. Grant didn't know when he would ever be ready for something so serious again.

As Grant walked Gertie out, Sonja and Derek flashed through his mind. If Derek had come by while they were at lunch, Derek would've had the opportunity to take the journal. But what would've been his motive? Grant didn't know Sonja and Derek very well on a personal level, but living in a small town means everybody knows your business. A few years his junior, Derek also grew up in Shady Springs Church.

Grant recalled Derek's home life being difficult. Derek's mother had bailed on him and his father when Derek was in grade school. His father spent more time with the bottle than with his family. He later died while Derek attended trade school. Derek met Sonja while at school, and they eventually married and came back to Shady Springs. Sonja started attending church a few months prior, literally dragging Derek with her. Grant chuckled to himself as he remembered Derek coming into the church with Sonja. Derek headed over to sit in the back, and Sonja stopped him and pulled him by the arm all the way to the front pew.

Go see him! a voice said within Grant, interrupting the memory.

It's getting kind of late, and they are probably having dinner. I could just call Derek tomorrow. Grant pushed the voice away.

Go see him! The voice pushed back. *Now!*

Okay, Lord, I'm going. Grant groaned within himself.

His flesh still tried to keep him from going. *Aren't you hungry? It's close to dinnertime. He doesn't even like you.*

It won't take long to stop by, and he might know something about the journal, he resolved to himself. He didn't know how Derek would react to his impromptu visit, but he knew better than to ignore the Lord's direction. He locked the church, hopped onto his bike, and revved it up.

Derek and Sonja lived in a new housing addition on the other side of the lake. It took him about ten minutes to get there. Derek and Sonja didn't have any children. Darlene once let it slip at the diner that Sonja had been upset because they'd been trying to no avail.

As he pulled into their driveway, he sent up a quick prayer. *Lord, give me the right words to say. Please let Derek's heart be receptive.* He knocked on the door and waited a few minutes till Derek answered.

"Oh, hey, Pastor," Derek said awkwardly. "We're kind of in the middle of dinner."

"That's alright, Derek. I don't want to intrude. I just wanted to check in with you guys on my way home today."

Derek looked confused. "Were you wanting to talk to Sonja? I can go get her instead if you want." He turned to make his escape.

"Actually, I came to talk to you," Grant said. Derek stopped in his tracks and turned back to Grant. Derek rubbed his neck and ran his hand through his hair. "Sonja came by the church today and said you might stop by. I'm afraid I might have missed you while out for lunch," Grant explained.

"Oh, yeah," Derek said as if he was suddenly remembering. "That's right. I did stop by. I looked in your office, but you weren't there, so I left."

I need to ask him about the journal, but I don't want to sound like I am accusing him. Grant decided to try a subtle approach. "Sorry, I missed you, man," he apologized. "I went out for lunch. I don't know if you heard or not, but Mercedes Lewis, the meteorologist, is in town investigating the cloud. Anyways, I found Pastor Hart's journal, and we were studying it for information before we took a lunch break."

At the mention of the journal, Derek glanced sideways and shifted nervously.

So, he does know something about it! Grant wanted to ask him more but noticed Sonja had crept behind

Derek and was quietly eavesdropping. "I don't want to take up a lot of your time now. Is there another time you want to come by the church to talk?" Grant asked instead.

Derek turned around and saw his wife. He sighed and turned back to Grant. "Sure, I guess I can come tomorrow on my lunch break."

"Awesome," Grant said, smiling. "Do you mind if we have a quick word of prayer before I go?"

Derek stammered, "Uh, okay, sure."

Grant bowed his head and prayed. "Lord, I want to thank you for bringing Sonja and Derek to our church. They have been such a blessing to me personally, to see them grow in you. I pray you bless their family as they seek your will. Strengthen and protect their marriage. Draw them closer to each other as they draw closer to You. Help them to put their faith and trust in You, Lord. Thank you for your blessings. In Jesus' name, Amen."

As Grant lifted his head, he noticed a brief softening in Derek's eyes. He decided he would wait and ask about the journal when they met. "I'll see you tomorrow. Don't forget about the volleyball game after church."

Sonja beamed as she said a quick thank you to Derek as she shut the door.

As Grant began his ride home, he reflected on his day. Although he didn't let on to Mercedes or Gertie, he was troubled by the incident with Gladys at the diner. *How many others in town are blaming me for the cloud's demise? What if I really am to blame? What if I'm not up to par with the other pastors before me?* Harold and Chase believed in him, but they were men. All men were fallible.

Grant wrestled with the doubt within himself all the way home. As he turned off his bike and opened the door to the parsonage the church provided for him, the realization hit him that it might not be his home for much longer. All he ever wanted to do was minister in Shady Springs. He wanted to give back to the people who had invested so much in his life. *If I'm not supposed to serve here, then where? Am I still called? Am I worthy of this calling?*

Grant went to the kitchen and opened the fridge. He pulled out some hamburger patties he made the night before and warmed them in the microwave. Then, he grabbed some whole wheat buns and cheese, mayo, and mustard. After a second thought, he grabbed some jalapeños too.

Grant took his burger and a glass of water to the couch. Before he started eating, he said out loud, "Lord, I don't know what's happening with my life right now, but I know You are the one holding the reins. Please show me the way."

As Derek Rossi brushed his teeth to get ready for bed, he thought back on Grant's visit. He felt guilty for taking the journal and wasn't sure what his next step should be. His original selfish intent planned to destroy it. However, if Grant and Ms. Lewis had already read the journal, then what would be the point? His secret would be out, and his marriage ruined. He rinsed off his toothbrush and put it in the medicine cabinet as Sonja came in and gave him a bear hug.

"What's that for?" Derek asked. Lately, the only time Sonja showed him any interest was for clinical procreating reasons.

"No reason," Sonja said as she kissed him on the cheek. "I'm just so thankful that we found a good church. I really appreciate you meeting with the pastor."

"Oh, yeah?" Derek said as he turned around and wrapped his arms around his wife.

"Mm-mm," Sonja murmured in his arms. "My parents had a really strong marriage. My mom always said it was because they based their marriage on God. I don't want to be another statistic of a failed marriage. I want us to last forever."

Derek tilted her head so he could gaze into her deep, dark brown eyes. "I will do whatever it takes to keep us together forever," he promised. He wrestled with a sudden onset of anxiety at the thought of losing her. He wondered how long Mercedes Lewis planned to stay in town. If she left sooner than later, perhaps the journal would be forgotten. Maybe she needed a little push to leave Shady Springs. It would be easy to find her; there was only one place to stay in their rinky-dink town. An idea began to form in his mind.

"What are you thinking about?" Sonja gazed at him suspiciously.

Derek gave her an impish grin and scooped her up, causing her to gasp in surprise.

"Derek!" Sonja squealed. Laughing, she wrapped her arms around his neck as he carried her into their bedroom.

8

MERCEDES

*I'm traveling through rough weather, and can only see
a few feet in front of me.*

—Mercedes

On her way back to her car, Mercedes pulled out her phone and noticed a few missed calls, one from her mother and one from her former boss. She decided to call her boss back first.

"Mercedes, I'm glad you called back! How is your cloud investigation going?" Reggie Thompson greeted her enthusiastically.

Mercedes filled Reggie in on the missing journal and the cloud's deterioration as she casually paced in front of her car outside the library.

"Mercedes, I think we should jump on this story while the cloud is still evident in the sky! I'm going to send a camera crew and let you do some freelance work. An inspirational piece, maybe? How does that sound?"

Mercedes' heart skipped. The prospect of a freelance job she could handle, but an inspirational piece? She didn't even know Reggie professed to be a Christian. Mercedes was not about to let this chance pass her by, though. "That sounds great! Just to clarify, you're okay with me mentioning the pastor and faith?"

"Of course! We can always edit out parts that may not resonate well with our viewers. Most people love a good inspirational story, though." Reggie told her the camera crew would be there first thing in the morning before hanging up.

Mercedes couldn't believe everything that had transpired. She sat on a bench in front of the library and quickly called her mother. Janet's voice turned to a shrill when she heard about her daughter's freelance job. She also expressed immense interest in Mercedes' afternoon with Pastor Grant.

Mercedes tried to downplay her afternoon with Grant; he was, after all, a pastor. *What do you know about being a pastor's wife? You think you are good enough for him?* Her self-doubt kicked in as more negative thoughts entered her mind. *Do you really want to deal with people like Gladys? You would be judged at every turn.*

By the time Mercedes finished talking with her mom, it was near 5:00 p.m. Mercedes got in her car and drove back to the B&B in disbelief of all that had happened to her that day. A small voice within her spoke softly. *Why do you continue to doubt? God has been with you each step on your journey. God's goodness unveils through your greatest trials.*

When Mercedes made it back to the inn, Bertie sat in the parlor with a pot of tea.

"I know it's technically past teatime, but would you like a cup, Mercedes?" offered Bertie.

"That would be fantastic. Thank you."

Bertie smiled as she poured the golden liquid in a dainty blue floral teacup. "Where there's tea, there is hope! Don't quote me on coming up with that, though; that's from a famous playwright, Sir Arthur Pinero. At least, I think that is who wrote it. Sometimes my brain is in a bit of a fog these days."

"I haven't heard that saying before, but I like it. There's nothing more comforting than a warm pot of tea."

"Did you find out anything interesting by the lake? Did you get a chance to meet Pastor Grant?" Bertie asked as she added a lump of sugar to her tea.

"Yes, and yes, to answer both your questions." Mercedes settled back to enjoy her tea. "Grant found Pastor Hart's journal from when he first traveled to Shady Springs. The diary verified the story that God led Pastor Hart's congregation to this town by a cloud. It seemed like they had a remarkable journey."

"And the cloud?" Bertie asked softly with a faraway glint in her eyes. "How did it look today?"

Mercedes recalled how upset Bertie seemed to get about the cloud topic yesterday. "It's still there," she assured her.

Bertie stood up from the table and pulled out an old photo album from a bookcase. She set the binder in front of Mercedes. "I've been photographing that cloud since I was a teenager. I have always been fascinated with it."

Curious, Mercedes opened up the album. Documented pictures of the cloud consumed each page. The first photo dated from May 1966. There was a picture of the cloud from each consecutive month of the year up until now. "Bertie, this is amazing!" Mercedes exclaimed, examining the pictures. The cloud currently diminished by half its size from the original photo; however, as Mercedes flipped through the glossy images, she noticed there was no reduction in the size of the cloud whatsoever until the photos from the beginning of the current year. "It looks as if the cloud began a noticeable change in size this January," Mercedes thought aloud as she scrutinized the photos closer. "Do you mind if I borrow your photo album to look through tonight? I might be able to use it in my news story tomorrow. The station is going to send a cameraman here to do an exposé."

"How exciting! A real cameraman?" Bertie stood, patting her hair. "I need to go see Rosie to fix my hairdo."

Mercedes smiled at the older woman's excitement. "Bertie, what made you photograph the cloud all these years?" The documentation would be very beneficial for her story, but to take photos for this long was slightly obsessive.

Bertie stopped reaching for her landline phone and turned around. "People said when evil came to our town, the cloud would leave. Evil came . . . I can't talk about it. I can't. I can't!" Bertie put her hands on her head and shook her head back and forth.

Alarmed, Mercedes rushed over and put her arm around her. "Bertie, you're okay. You're safe," she said, trying to calm her. She grabbed the phone and showed it to her. "Do you still want to get your hair done? Remember, you were going to call Rosie to fix your hair?" *God, please let Gertie come back soon!* Mercedes thought to herself. She had no idea what she should do.

Bertie let go of her head and peered up toward Mercedes. "Rosie?"

"Yes," Mercedes hesitated. "Do you remember her number?"

Bertie sniffed and waved her hand behind her. "Gertie writes the numbers down for me."

Mercedes followed her gesture and saw a list of numbers on the wall. Bertie handed Mercedes the phone. "I think I better go lie down. I'm not feeling very well."

"Do you need help?"

Bertie looked at Mercedes like she was the crazy one. "To lie down? I think not!" Bertie huffed and walked down the hallway and went into what Mercedes gathered was her bedroom.

Mercedes cleaned the tea service, picked up the photo album, and retired to her bedroom. As she opened the door to her room, an envelope fluttered to the floor. Intrigued, Mercedes scooped it off the floor. She laid the binder on the bedside table and carefully opened the letter. Wide-eyed, she began to read.

Mercedes Lewis,

You are not who everyone thinks you are. Leave our town and stay out of our bizness! If you don't, you will be sorry!!

The note was typed on regular copy paper. Mercedes studied the envelope, but it was blank. *Well, this is a bizarre turn of events*, Mercedes thought. *Who would want to threaten me?* Mercedes noticed the spelling errors in the note and wondered if the person who invited her here in the first place had now changed their mind.

The room phone rang, causing her to jump. "Hello?" Mercedes tried to keep her voice calm. Her trepidation faded as Gertie's cheerful voice spoke through the phone.

"Hello, dear! I just wanted to let you know that dinner will be ready in fifteen minutes. We are having lasagna and salad. Cheesecake for dessert."

"That sounds wonderful," Mercedes said. "I'll be right down."

Mercedes hung up the phone in a whirlwind of thoughts and went to the bathroom to freshen up. What she really wanted to do was climb into the clawfoot tub and turn into a raisin. She sighed, hoping dinner wouldn't take too long.

On the way down the staircase, Mercedes ran into Hap. *What if he's my creeper?* Hap seemed like a nice enough old man, but Mercedes didn't really know him. *Then again, I don't really know anyone here.* "Have you heard if anyone else has checked in to the B&B?" Maybe he had seen someone.

"I wouldn't know. I just got back from house hunting."

"Have you had any luck?" Mercedes asked.

"As a matter of fact, yes. I signed the contract today." Hap's eyes gleamed with excitement.

"That's awesome! Congratulations!"

They followed the smell of garlic and parmesan into the dining room. Mercedes fixed her plate at the sideboard and sat to eat. Her appetite waned as she stared across at Bernie's empty chair at the table. "Is Bertie feeling okay?" she asked Gertie.

"I checked on her earlier, and she said she felt tired. I'll bring her a plate later."

Mercedes wanted to fill Gertie in with what happened with Bertie; however, she didn't feel comfortable discussing it with Hap around. Gertie herself seemed uncharacteristically quiet at the table.

"Hap has some exciting news to share," Mercedes offered, breaking the silence at the table.

Hap told the women about the house he settled on buying. He pulled out his phone and showed them a few pictures of a pristine log cabin nestled near the lake with a fishing dock. The owner threw his fishing boat in to seal the deal. Mercedes couldn't tell if Hap was more excited about the cabin or the boat.

"As a matter of fact," Hap said, confirming Mercedes' thoughts, "I think I'm going to go to do some online shopping for some new fishing gear. If you ladies will excuse me?"

They said goodnight to Hap, and Mercedes began to help Gertie clear the table.

"Put those plates down!" scolded Gertie. "You are supposed to be our guest."

Mercedes pretended she didn't hear her and followed her into the kitchen. "Gertie, I think I'm the reason for Bertie not feeling well tonight." *Might as well come out with it.*

"Whatever do you mean?" Gertie set her rag down and turned to Mercedes.

"Earlier this evening, Bertie invited me to sit for some tea. She showed me her cloud photo album. When I asked her the reason why she took so many pictures, she got upset. Bertie kept saying that evil came, and she couldn't talk about it. I got her to calm down, but something I said seemed to rattle her." Mercedes set the plates in the soapy water.

Gertie pursed her lips and returned to washing the dishes. Mercedes hoped that she would offer an explanation, but all she mentioned was Bertie had trouble with her memory and not to take much stock in what she said. Their mother had died while the girls were young, and Gertie had to watch her sister while their dad worked. They attended school until the sixth grade. Gertie paused in thought.

"What is it? Do you remember something?"

"I forgot. It happened so long ago." Gertie scrubbed harder on the lasagna pan, then set it down and turned to Mercedes with tears in her eyes. "What year did Bertie start taking those pictures?" Gertie asked.

"1966, I think," Mercedes said. "Did something significant happen that year?"

"In 1966, Bertie suffered greatly." Gertie dried her hands and motioned for Mercedes to follow her back into the dining room. They both sat at the table, facing each other. "We had jobs at the chicken house that summer. We hated working there. The heat scorched our skin with an unbearable stench, and our boss was a wicked man. We worked there for about a year. I was eighteen, and Bertie was sixteen. One day I couldn't go in—I felt ill. I tried to get Bertie to stay home with me, but she wouldn't. She was saving her money for a car and said she could take care of herself. Bertie came home that evening crying, her dress torn. That evil man raped her. My father tried to press charges, but they said it would be his word against hers." Gertie rubbed her temples as she continued. "It was an awful year. Bertie got pregnant as a result but miscarried. Thankfully, that horrible man moved his family up north, so we didn't have to see his face anymore."

"How terrible for Bertie. Do you think that when she mentioned evil coming, she was referring to what happened to her all those years ago?"

"It's possible. Our pastor at that time preached using fear as a motivator. I didn't particularly care for him. He would say that if our town fell to the ways of sin, God would take away His blessing from us, and the cloud would be gone."

"So, she started taking pictures of the cloud in fear that what happened to her would cause it to go away," Mercedes surmised. "No wonder she's been so upset. But that happened so long ago. Surely, she can't think that event is what's driving the cloud's dispersing?"

Gertie shook her head. "I have no idea. I'll have to speak to her about it tomorrow."

Mercedes told Gertie about the cameraman coming the next morning and hoped it wouldn't cause Bertie any more agitation. She trudged up the stairs to her room and prepared her bath. As the tub filled, Mercedes' mind went back to the threatening note and realized she'd forgotten to tell Gertie about it. She considered calling her mom, but she didn't want to worry her. *I don't think I can handle a conversation with anyone else tonight. I feel like I'm treading water, and every time I think I've got something to hold on to for support, it suddenly slips away. I need to get focused on one thing.* She flopped on her bed and picked up the Bible on the nightstand—those cast iron tubs took forever to fill. The Bible fell open to Psalms 27. *Strange, I know I've read this chapter before lots of times, but I don't remember these verses.* Her eyes zeroed in on verses seven through nine (KJV).

> *Hear, O LORD, when I cry with my voice: have mercy also upon me, and answer me.*
> *When thou saidst, Seek ye my face; my heart said unto thee, Thy face, LORD, will I seek.*
> *Hide not thy face far from me; put not thy servant away in anger: thou hast been my help; leave me not, neither forsake me, O God of my salvation.*

A voice within her spoke. *David himself had times of doubt, fear, and abandonment. I'm right here with you.* Tears welled in Mercedes' eyes. Mercedes whispered, "I know, Lord. I want to seek you again. Help me see you in my life. Show me who to trust. I'm scared. I'm traveling through rough weather, and I can only see a few feet in front of me. I need you." As Mercedes spoke those last words resolutely, she felt more pieces of her wall crumbling as she finally admitted to herself that she could no longer go through this journey alone.

The bathtub was mostly full, so Mercedes got up from her bed and took a much-needed soak in the tub. She allowed the warm water to soothe her mind and body. Finally, with her body relaxed and her mind completely exhausted, Mercedes collapsed under the quilt on her bed and fell into a deep sleep.

It seemed as soon as she shut her eyes, her alarm went off. Groaning, she buried herself under the covers.

Then, remembering the camera crew coming, she threw off the covers and scrambled out of bed. She pulled out a navy knee-length skirt and a lilac cardigan set she'd hung up the night before and laid them on her bed. Luckily, they didn't need ironing. Mercedes hated ironing. She did her makeup and her hair while she was still in her pajamas. She just needed to get dressed when the landline phone rang.

"Hello?" Mercedes asked as she checked her hair again in the mirror.

"Hey, Mercedes. It's Grant. Did I wake you?"

"Oh, hi, Grant. No, you didn't wake me. Did you get the journal back?" Mercedes sat on the bed and began playing with a strand of hair.

"No, not yet. I think I know who took it. I'm hoping I'll know more later today. I was calling to ask you if you would mind playing in our volleyball game tonight after church? We're short a player and could really use you."

"Well, I don't think I would be very much help. I haven't played in years," Mercedes said with a laugh.

"It's strictly for fun. None of us are that good. We are just trying to help the youth practice for church camp."

"I was actually planning on leaving tonight." Mercedes hesitated.

"Oh," Grant said. Mercedes could hear the dejection in his voice.

What would one more night hurt? She asked herself. *You might need to stay another night, depending on what direction Reggie decides to take with your story.* "You know what? I think I am going to stay another night. I might need to stay longer for more information for the story. They are sending a cameraman to Shady Springs this morning, and we're going to film some shots of the town."

"Awesome! So, you will be able to come?"

Mercedes said she would, then had an idea. "We could probably use a few shots of the church. Would you mind if I brought the cameraman over there this morning?"

"Sure," Grant said.

Mercedes said she would text him when they headed over that way. Grant gave her his number, and she entered it into her phone. As she hung up the phone, she saw the Bible lying next to it. She picked it up and opened it to the Psalms. Psalms 9:19 (KJV): *And they that know thy name will put their trust in thee: for thou, LORD, hast not forsaken them that seek thee.*

"Help me, Lord, to see you today. Show me the way I should go and the people to trust." Mercedes prayed again as she got dressed. She pulled out her laptop and began to organize her thoughts. First, what were the facts? She had visual data, thanks to Bertie. Then, there was written evidence of the cloud's first sighting in 1850. That meant the cloud had been in existence for around 170 years. Clouds were always changing shape, morphing into something new. This cloud was scientifically impossible.

The journal attributed the cloud to God as an indication of His presence and guidance. Mercedes thought it was interesting that each person had a personal connection with the cloud. Judd Hart's daughter and different townspeople each felt that the cloud was there for them personally. Some thought of it as a symbol of hope or direction from God, and others, a comforting reminder of a loved one.

What is your personal connection with the cloud? something within her asked.

Mercedes dismissed the thought. *I'm only here for the story.* Certainly, she felt intrigued by the cloud, but she was not having her own interaction with it. *You have already had interaction.* The voice clarified, *Look at what God is doing with your relationship. Look how God is bringing you back to Him.*

Mercedes blinked in surprise. "Is that really what's happening here?" she asked aloud. She shook her head and relented to herself that perhaps it was. She asked to see God working in her life, yet she kept pushing Him away. "Alright, Lord. If you could only help me get this story done, I promise I won't block you out anymore."

9

GRANT

Just keep looking to Him and be ready!

—*Roy George*

When Grant got up the next morning, he received a text from a church member that they were sick and weren't going to make it to church that night. That also meant they weren't going to be able to play in the volleyball game after the service. The game wasn't that big of a deal, but he got an inkling that perhaps Mercedes might want to play. It would open the door to get her to attend the evening service as well.

Grant decided to give Mercedes a call. *I left her number on my desk at the church.* He would have to call her at the hotel via Gertie. Grant found Gertie's contact info on his phone, pressed the call button, and groaned. *This is going to be all over town, courtesy of my senior saints.*

When Mercedes first answered, it didn't sound like she would make it, and a feeling of disappointment washed over him. In fact, he was surprised how let down he felt at the thought of not seeing her. After Mercedes agreed to come and ended the call, Grant sighed in relief and whistled to himself as he fixed a bowl of Raisin Bran®. Grant's buddies in Bible college called him an old man because of his favorite cereal. He couldn't help but love the crunchy flakes and chewy bits of sweetness from the raisins.

Grant reminisced on his Bible college days while he finished eating. He had one friend, Randy, who would always fall asleep in class. One time, while the professor lectured, they elbowed Randy, who had unwittingly fallen asleep, and told him the professor asked him to stand and pray. Randy jumped up and started praying right in the middle of class, much to the amusement of his classmates and the professor. Grant also had a dorm parent named Roy George, who had a prosthetic arm. Roy would remove his prosthetic while sleeping, then wake up to find it in the oddest places, like the refrigerator or flagpole. Grant almost choked on his cereal as he remembered when someone placed his friend's prosthetic arm on the door to the dean's office.

The walk down memory lane made Grant realize that he hadn't heard from Roy George in a while. Roy had married and taken a church near Hamburg, Arkansas. Grant trusted Roy's advice and decided to give him a call.

Roy answered immediately. "Hey, man! How's it going?"

"Good. I hadn't heard from you in a while, so I thought I'd give you a call."

"It's kind of funny you would call. I was thinking about you the other day. Are you still with the church at Shady Springs?"

"I am. I don't know for how much longer, but I am for right now." Grant took a deep breath and told Roy about the cloud and the church elders.

"So, let me get all of this straight. This cloud has been hovering over the lake since the time of the founding pastor?"

"Yep."

"And now it's disappearing?"

"Right."

"And they think you are the reason for this?"

Grant sighed. "It seems that way. I'm not sure what to say or do at this point. It's so crazy."

"Well, it may not be for us to know how or why God left the cloud there all this time. It kind of sucks for you, brother, but all you can control is your own relationship with the Lord. The townspeople need to realize that God wants a relationship with each of them. If their heads are in the cloud and not in Him, that might be why He is taking their safety blanket away."

"So, what should I do?" Grant could feel his voice start to choke. The thought of leaving his congregation and his family nearly broke him.

"Listen—pray up. Stay humble. God isn't finished with you yet. This is all a part of a greater plan or purpose for your life. I do know there is a church near Magnolia needing an interim pastor. This might be the reason the Lord put you on my mind. Keep praying about the Lord's direction in your life. Tozer said, 'God takes the initiative to provide direction for your life.' Just keep looking to Him and be ready."

As Grant ended the call with Roy, he felt ten times lighter. Next, he called Harold and told him about the news story. The lawn and building of the church were well maintained, but they would want to make sure it looked as nice as possible for the camera. Harold said he would call Chase, and they'd take care of it. Grant grabbed the keys to his truck and drove to meet them at the church.

When Grant arrived at the church, Harold and Chase were huddled together, talking. "Hey, guys, what do you think? Are we camera ready?" Grant approached them, smiling. His smile faded when he saw the grim expressions on their faces. "What's wrong?" Grant asked with a sigh.

"It's the town elders," Harold replied, making a face. "They got their panties all in a wad because they were not given proper notice of being in the news."

"It's not like we held it back from them. We scarcely found out about this ourselves," Grant protested.

"The elders want to know what the intention of the newscast is before they give permission for the story. They don't want Pastor Hart or Shady Springs ridiculed," Chase explained.

"Permission?" Grant repeated incredulously. "I'm fairly sure the news station doesn't require permission from the town elders! Anyway, Mercedes is running the story, and she said it's a faith piece, sort of an inspirational spin. No one is going to be made a fool."

Harold's ears perked at the familiar tone in which Grant referred to Mercedes. "Mercedes Lewis, is it? The cute little weather girl on Channel 2?"

Grant rolled his eyes. "She's a meteorologist, Harold, a scientist. She'd probably knock you out for referring to her as a little weather girl. And yes, she is the one doing the story. So, you can tell the town elders there's nothing to fear. Mercedes is a Christian, and she isn't out to make a mockery of the church."

While the three were talking, a white King Ranch Ford truck zoomed into the drive. Grant recognized the owner of the truck right away as Sammie Telford, mayor of Shady Springs. Harold raised his eyebrows at Grant as Chase left to smooth things over with the elders.

"Pastor Grant, Harold," the mayor acknowledged them both with a head nod.

Although Grant had a lot of respect for the fiery, petite woman, he hadn't had a lot of dealings with Mayor Telford. *Oops*, Grant mentally corrected himself, *she prefers the title Mayor Sammie.*

Sammie Telford was a member of the African Methodist Episcopal Church in the neighboring town of Cedar Ridge. It made quite the headline when she won the election, beating out the most recent male offspring of the Rutledge family. The Rutledge family had passed the mayor title down their lineage for the past twenty years. When Mayor Sammie won, the town seemed to have finally shaken itself awake. Grant was astonished she remembered his name and even more so that she knew Harold. "I heard Shady Springs was going to be in the news! Is this correct?" she asked.

Grant thought, *At least she's excited about it, unlike some other people.* "That's right, Mayor Sammie." Grant explained, "Mercedes Lewis is going to do an exposé on our cloud and town history, a story of faith."

"That should be a very interesting piece coming from a meteorologist perspective. If she has any questions about the town history or would like a mayoral perspective, I would like to make myself available to her."

"It will be an hour or so before she makes it over here. You're welcome to wait here or at the diner."

"Well, it's been a while since I had Darlene's homemade cinnamon rolls." Mayor Sammie's eyes danced as she made eyes at Harold. "Care to join me?"

As Harold declined in lieu of getting the church ready, Grant stood stupefied, wondering how he could have missed that development.

Mayor Sammie drove away, and Grant sent Mercedes a text about the Mayor's offer. He then went inside to make some phone calls. After checking in with Ryan about his newborn baby, Grant's phone rang. Derek Rossi's name lit the screen. "Hey, Derek! How's it going, man?"

"It's going good, Pastor. Are you still able to meet during my lunch break? It would be around noon."

"That sounds fine. I'll see you then!" Grant hung up the phone and said a silent prayer. *Lord, please give me the words to say to reach him. I don't know for sure what his and Sonja's issue is, but you do. Soften his heart; help him be receptive.* As Grant prayed, Mercedes' face came to his mind. *Lord be with Mercedes today and with her story. Help her story bless others and be a testament to Your faithfulness. Heal whatever wounds she may have against You or the church.*

As if on cue, Grant's phone pinged with a message from Mercedes. *Cameraman here. Shooting a few shots at B&B and then will be over. Maybe an hour.*

Okay. Grant checked the time as he texted back. It was 10:00 a.m. He stretched and walked over to the fellowship hall to start a pot of coffee. As he pulled a mug out, Gladys and a few other ladies came scurrying into the building. Harold and Chase entered behind them.

"Pastor Grant, is it true? Is Mercedes Lewis going to do a story at our church this morning?" Gladys demanded.

"She sure is. I just got a text that she will be here in an hour."

"One hour?" Gladys repeated incredulously. "That's not enough time to get everything ready. We need the new flower arrangements out, and we need to polish the pews!"

"*Oooh*, what if we used our patriotic flower arrangement? Is it too early for Memorial Day?" One of the ladies interrupted Gladys, and the other ladies all started chiming in, chatting excitedly.

Grant suppressed a smile. Those ladies drove him crazy, but their enthusiasm warmed his heart.

Harold rolled his eyes and clutched his heart dramatically, "Oh, Chase. What flowers are we going to put out front? Zinnias or petunias? It's so hard to know!"

Chase did a little hop and clapped his hands. "Is it too early for the manger scene? It has such a dramatic effect."

Grant turned around to pour his coffee so he wouldn't burst out laughing and offend his ladies.

"Harold Martin and Chase Westin!" Gladys scolded. "That is not funny! You men have been single for too long. You have completely forgotten your manners!"

Harold and Chase were also the most eligible bachelors in the church for the sixty-and-up crowd. Harold had thwarted Gladys's efforts thus far, but she hadn't given up trying to snag him.

Gladys turned on her heels to the ladies and gave them the charge. "Let's go, ladies. We've got work to do!" The ladies buzzed around their queen bee out the door toward the church building.

Harold and Chase chuckled, grabbed some mugs, and joined Grant around the coffee pot.

"You guys are so bad," Grant said, shaking his head. "I don't think Gladys is going to give up on you, Harold. You boys think y'all will ever settle down again?"

Chase shook his head. "Not me. Don't get me wrong—I loved my wife and being married. It took me a long time to get over her death and get used to being on my own again. Let's just say I am happy with my life the way it is now."

"And what about you, Harold? What was going on with the mayor back there?" Grant asked.

"Well, when Mayor Sammie first took office, I went to see her to set a few things straight with her about our town."

"And?" Grant prompted.

Harold chuckled. "Mayor Sammie set me straight about a few things. Now, we are old friends." He changed the subject back to Grant. "What about you and this Mercedes Lewis? Is there anything happening there?"

Grant shrugged with a half-smile. "I have to admit, I'm intrigued with her and would like to get to know her better."

Chase set his coffee down. "I know that since Nat died, it's been hard for you to even think about having another relationship. It's been four years now, though. She would want you to move on and be happy."

Grant stared down in his coffee cup. "Nat and I had our life mapped out. We had one more year of Bible college, and then we were going to start our ministry together. When she died suddenly in that car collision, those dreams were wrecked. It's hard to have that hope again once you've had it stripped away."

"It is hard," Chase agreed. "But God has another beautiful plan for you, Grant, if you are ready to give to Him."

Grant sighed. "I know. I'm trying."

Chase patted him on the shoulder, and the three men sipped their coffee in comfortable silence.

Derek Rossi stared at the blinking line on his computer screen. He had just closed out a job ticket for a client and debated whether to pull up another help ticket or stop for lunch. Deciding to stay in the good graces of his wife, Derek logged out of his computer and took his lunch break. Before he left, he had to make a phone call to the B&B. They had one of those old dial-up phones, so he wasn't worried about caller ID. *It's basically a prank call*, he reasoned within himself. No harm, no foul. He still didn't know what he would say to Mercedes Lewis to discourage her from her quest.

He practiced a low, scratchy voice. "Get out of town." *Stupid*, he thought. "Leave now before you get hurt." He groaned. *Do I really want to sound like a bad guy?*

When the phone rang a few times with no answer, Derek breathed a sigh of relief. *Really dumb idea. At least she didn't pick up.*

As he drove over to the church, Derek contemplated his next course of action. He knew what he should do, but he wasn't sure if he was man enough to do it. *What would my father do? My old man probably wouldn't have cared enough to take the journal.* That wasn't really fair. His dad had cared up till his mom left. Then, his dad just stopped living. Derek was hit with the sudden realization that in all of his trying to not be like his dad, he had ended up just like him. *I've made Sonja my reason for living. If she left me right now, I would end up exactly like my dad. What am I missing? Maybe I can talk to Grant about it.*

Derek passed the diner and noticed a commotion coming from the church. Derek swore as he saw a police car and a news crew. Heck, even the mayor was there.

He found out his journal was missing and called the cops! Derek thought to himself.

Panic began to overtake him as he realized they were probably waiting for his appearance to arrest him. He pressed the gas, ducked down, and sped past the church. No way he was going there now.

Derek drove straightaway to his office, checking his rearview mirror every so often to ensure no one followed him. When he arrived back to the safety of his office parking lot, he sat in his car for a moment and pulled out his phone. "Hey, Pastor Grant, I'm not going to be able to make it this afternoon after all," Derek tried to speak in a calm, even tone.

"Oh, sorry to hear that, Derek," Grant replied.

Derek thought he detected a hint of disappointment in Grant's voice and felt a pang of regret. He kind of felt like he hit a breakthrough or something. *What if the moment passes, and I stay stuck where I am? What if I can't get any of this stuff inside me resolved?* "Yeah, a thing at work came up. Are you very busy today? Maybe we can reschedule?" Derek fished around to see if Grant would give up the earlier goings-on at the church.

"Actually, things are pretty crazy at the church right now anyway," Grant admitted. "Mercedes Lewis is doing a story on our cloud, and the whole town got wind of it. Everybody, including the mayor, is trying to get in the story." He ended with a laugh.

"Sounds like you have your hands full there. Let me check my schedule again, and I will get back to you on another time to meet."

"Sounds good, Derek," Grant agreed.

As Derek ended the call, relief flooded over him that there was a reasonable explanation for what was occurring at the church parking lot. Nobody was onto him, and he wasn't going to jail. If only he could come up with a reasonable explanation of why he had taken that blasted journal.

His thoughts again turned to Mercedes Lewis. *If only she would just leave.* All of this chaos seemed to be centered around her. It's time for Ms. Lewis to leave Shady Springs once and for all.

Grant truly felt disappointed that Derek didn't show up for their meeting, but he didn't exaggerate when he told Derek that everyone in town had shown up.

The church looked like a complete circus. His quiet coffee group of three only lasted a few moments until it exploded into a chaotic sideshow.

Grant was impressed with how Mercedes Lewis handled everything and everyone. She was professional and courteous. When she spoke to people, she made them feel valued. Mercedes did an interview with the mayor and the police chief. She also answered questions from different townspeople who stopped by. When Mercedes walked into the sanctuary, she noticed the different florals and commented to Gladys and the other ladies how nice the building looked.

As they finished their interviews, Mercedes and the camera crew were ushered into the church auditorium by Gladys and the other women. The ladies had managed to put out a little sandwich and dessert spread for their distinguished guests. Mercedes gushed about how delicious everything tasted and how thoughtful the ladies were. Grant reminded everyone of the evening service as they ate. Eventually, Mercedes left with the camera crew back to the hotel with a promise she'd return later that evening for the service.

Grant offered to help Gladys and the other ladies clean up, but they quickly shooed him away. He bid the ladies adieu and went back to his office to do some more studying.

However, focusing on his sermon proved challenging. He kept going back to the interviews Mercedes had done with the town elders. Although they were enamored with Mercedes and her news story, they were none too pleased by the cloud's further demise. Grant remembered word for word what Elder Harper told Mercedes while giving Grant the evil eye.

"In all of our town and church history, this cloud has remained. One has to wonder why we are losing our heritage and faith now." Elder Harper's tall and lanky frame stooped over Mercedes. The cameraman almost fell in the lake as he moved backward to fit him in the frame.

Mercedes reminded the man that faith was not by sight, and everyone else in the world depended on blind faith.

The man backstepped and said they'd still have faith without the cloud. "God, of course, is bigger than the cloud. It still doesn't explain why God wanted what served as a source of comfort to so many of their townspeople to depart from them now. There must be some reason for this consequence." Elder Harper pointed emphatically at Grant.

Despite Mercedes' advocacy, Grant knew he still ranked low on the totem pole with the deacon board and council members. Unable to shake his sense of foreboding, he went for a walk to try and clear his head.

10

MERCEDES

*Fear holds us back from God's blessings because fear
keeps us from walking by faith.*

—Grant

Since Mercedes had done all the research and had a list of key shots by the time the editor and cameraman arrived, the filming was a breeze. She had worked with Frank, the cameraman, on her weather team before. Her editor was a young Hispanic woman named Gabrielle. Mercedes knew little about her except she turned down Tucker, which made the woman alright in Mercedes' mind.

Frank and Gabrielle arrived in time for breakfast. They mapped out their day over sausage, eggs, and fresh fruit. Bertie seemed to be in a good frame of mind. Mercedes interviewed her about the cloud photos. Bertie had one strange moment toward the end of the interview.

"Things will be made right again, and the cloud will continue. I am going to rid the evil from our town." Bertie jutted her chin out with a crazed look in her eye, and Mercedes decided to end the interview at that point. She was still trying to figure out what Bertie was talking about when she received a text from Grant about the mayor.

Mercedes told Gabrielle about the mayor wanting an interview, and Gabrielle got excited. "This could add more credibility to your story," she said as she added the interview down on their shot list.

They packed up the equipment and headed out to the church. On their way out, Mercedes texted Grant to let him know they were coming.

As they drew near to the church, a whole caravan awaited them. There were several cars in the parking lot, including a patrol car and different people milling about excitedly. The cloud floated stationary over the lake, heedless of the events taking place beneath it. Mercedes snapped a picture of it on her phone and compared it with the one taken the day before. The cloud had decreased in size again.

Grant stepped out of the crowd to greet her. Mercedes felt a calmness wash over her as she walked toward him. "Wow, this turned out to be quite the event." Mercedes gestured to the crowd behind him.

"I think everyone and their cousin is here," Grant said with a laugh.

The crowd hung back in awe as Gabrielle and Frank began to unload the equipment. Mercedes recognized Gladys standing in the background with some of the other ladies from the restaurant. A sharply dressed black woman came up to them and introduced herself as Mayor Sammie. She was very welcoming and complimentary. They decided to conduct the mayor's interview first over by the lake.

Sammie Telford had been born and raised in Shady Springs. She told of how her great-grandmother was a cook for the Rutherford family back when the family still held office. If only her great-grandmother could see her now—her grandbaby girl—the mayor.

When Mercedes asked her about what the cloud personally represented to her, Sammie paused and got a little teary-eyed. "I'm a morning person, you see. I rise up early, fix some coffee, and start my day with my Bible on my porch. It may seem silly to some, but during that morning quiet time, I gaze out at that cloud, and it's like God is right there just for me, listening to me. The cloud reminds me when I go out for the day God is right there with me."

Mercedes asked her what she thought about the cloud's slow withdrawal.

"I think that perhaps God is ready to see what kind of faith the townspeople of Shady Springs really have. Hopefully, we don't disappoint Him," the mayor replied with a small smile and a shrug.

Mercedes couldn't believe how well the interview had gone. Sammie Telford carried herself beautifully and was simply inspiring. She sent a questioning look to Gabrielle and received an enthusiastic thumbs up.

As Mercedes thanked Mayor Sammie, Gabrielle had Frank shoot some footage of the lake and church. Grant introduced her first to the police chief, who happened to be a fan, then to a man whose lineage went back to the original settlers of the town. The man was definitely one of the townspeople who blamed the cloud's departure on Pastor Grant. Even though she didn't particularly like the man, she did realize something as she spoke with him. It was a thought that had been staring at her in the face for a long time, simple yet profound. The townspeople of Shady Springs had grown dependent on this physical manifestation of God for hope, comfort, and assurance. Fear of facing trials without a physical presence or assurance was daunting for every Christian in their walk with God. It was easy to observe God in the good times when the blessings were abounding; it was a lot harder to find God under duress. Those times of uncertainty and difficulty were where faith was required.

Gladys approached her, interrupting her thoughts. Mercedes remembered the incident in the diner the previous day and tensed, not knowing what to expect. *Wait a minute. Gladys and Gertie are friends. She probably has access to the inn. Could Gladys have left the threatening note?* Much to her relief, Gladys was pleasant and invited them to a light lunch in the fellowship hall. On their way to the fellowship hall, Mercedes knew she had made a new best friend after mentioning the flower arrangements.

When everyone sat down to eat in the fellowship hall, Mercedes intentionally sat by Grant. She wanted to show him the note she received, but there hadn't been a good time. Mercedes still hadn't told anyone about the threat. Honestly, so much had happened it had been hard to process. An overwhelming sense of pressure built up within her that this could be more than just a threat, and she should take it seriously.

While everyone ate, Harold asked how she heard about their town. "It's a bit of a mystery. I received an email from an anonymous person about the cloud. It intrigued me, so I decided to come and investigate." Mercedes didn't mention that she lost her job at the station and had a lot of spare time to fill as well. She had braced herself in case she might have to explain to people that she was no longer on the weather team. Thankfully, the subject wasn't broached.

Mercedes opened the email on her phone and handed it to Harold to read. "Sound like anyone you know?" she said, half-joking, half-serious.

"No, although the speech reminds me of an older person," Harold thoughtfully said as he handed her back the phone.

Gabrielle reminded them they still had about three hours of editing to do. They ate their last few bites and headed back to the hotel. Mercedes decided she would show Grant the note after church later that night. *What could happen between now and then?* she thought to herself.

When they pulled into the B&B, Gabrielle rubbed her hands together eagerly. She raised her eyebrows at them. "Time for the magic to happen!"

Mercedes laughed while Frank groaned.

"Do you have to say that every time?" Frank grumbled.

Gabrielle replied to Frank with a wink. "Yep. It's my job. I take your mess and make a masterpiece!"

Mercedes was still smiling as she bounded the stairs to her room to freshen up. She'd enjoyed working with Frank and Gabrielle. They were fun and easy to collaborate with. Her smile faded, however, when she found her room ajar. Her clothes and notes were scattered across the floor.

A note laid open on her bed, written in an angry red. "Go away! This is your last chance!"

Mercedes stared in disbelief and hugged herself. She felt violated and angry that someone had been through and touched her things. She also felt confused and scared as to why this vehemence was shown toward her. *I don't have time for this.* "Just concentrate on finishing the editing job and then get the heck out of this town!" Mercedes mumbled to herself as she wiped away a few hot, angry tears.

Mercedes took a deep breath and picked up the landline. Gertie immediately came upstairs and stood flabbergasted when she saw the state of Mercedes' room. She apologized profusely. "I can't imagine why anybody would do this! And to you of all people!" Gertie exclaimed.

Mercedes showed Gertie the earlier note as Frank and Gabrielle popped their heads in the doorway. "What's all the commotion—" Gabrielle stopped short as she surveyed the state of Mercedes' dishevelled accommodations.

Frank let out a low whistle and said, "Someone's not happy with you being here."

Gabrielle concurred and asked Mercedes how much longer she planned on staying.

"I'm leaving tomorrow morning," Mercedes replied firmly.

They helped her pick up her things and headed to the dining room, where Gertie allowed them to work on the editing. By five o'clock, they had edited about two hours of footage down to a little over two minutes. Gabrielle and Frank still had work to do at the station, so they said their goodbyes. As they left, they committed Mercedes to call them in the morning when she left.

The church service didn't begin until seven, and Mercedes felt exhausted. She went up to her room to try to nap, but sleep evaded her. *Who's threatening me? Is it the same person who stole the journal?* She tossed and turned until she sat up exasperated. "Why am I even still here?" she whispered. She was scared to admit the real reason to herself. It wasn't totally about the cloud or her job anymore. It was also about a motorcycle riding, mustache-wearing preacher man. That revelation absolutely terrified her. Crowds she could do. Cameras she could do—relationships she could not. She considered packing her bags right then and there and heading out of town. "No one would blame me; I'm being threatened," Mercedes said out loud as if defending her cowardice would help.

She sighed, got up, and fixed her hair again for church. Mercedes headed downstairs. *I should have asked Grant what the ladies wore at his church. Too late to change now.*

She felt her level of anxiety rise as she left the inn and neared the white chapel. She turned off the engine and sat in the parking lot. *You can still leave. Nobody has seen you yet,* she thought.

Someone rapped on her window, smashing through her thoughts. Mercedes looked up in panic and was flooded with relief when she saw Gladys at her car door. Mercedes smiled and stepped out of the car.

"Sorry, I didn't mean to startle you," the older woman apologized.

"That's alright," Mercedes replied as they began to walk into the building. Mercedes was glad to walk in with Gladys. It was hard to walk into a church as a visitor, much less someone who had some things to clear up with God. *I guess I'm a backslidden Christian.* Mercedes winced at the thought. It hurt to think of herself that way, but the time had come to admit to herself where she stood in her spiritual walk. She had grown stagnant in her faith, but she was determined to find her way back.

The number of people in attendance surprised Mercedes. There were probably around fifty people already gathered, and she was about ten minutes early.

Grant stood with some of the youth talking and smiled at her as she approached. "Here comes our secret weapon now." Grant pointed to her as he taunted the teens. "You kids are going down!"

A tall boy with curly, red hair said, "I hope you remembered your BENGAY®, Pastor Grant! You're going to be so sore tonight." The young people around him laughed.

"Haha, you're so funny, Wendell, I forgot to laugh!" Grant retorted.

The kids all rolled their eyes and groaned. Mercedes tried not to smile at the corny line.

"That joke is so old," Wendell said, "just like Pastor Grant!" The kids all started laughing again.

"Come on," Grant whispered to Mercedes. "Let's get out of here before I bury myself deeper."

As they walked away from the youth, Mercedes worried about Grant's expectations of her volleying skills. "You know I haven't played in a long time, right?" If he thought she was going to be that much help on the team, he was going to be very disappointed.

"Yeah, I like to get them riled up a bit," Grant said.

"Well, I've been rather riled up today as well." Mercedes proceeded to tell Grant about the afternoon incident and the note from yesterday.

As Grant listened, his jaw dropped in disbelief. "Someone got in your room? That isn't safe, Mercedes! Did you call the cops?"

"I didn't think they would do anything. Nothing was taken, and there wasn't anything specific enough in the notes for the police to take action. Anyway, I'm planning on leaving for my parent's house in the morning."

"I can't believe someone from our town would do that to you. I know most everybody here, and it seems unfathomable."

"Yes. Besides the stolen journal, being called out at the diner, and then being threatened, everyone has been so nice," she said with a hint of sarcasm.

"Well, when you put it that way, I guess this town has been kind of rough on you. You probably regret coming here." Grant gave her a sympathetic smile.

"I admit. It has been a rough couple of days. But I've seen a true miracle with that cloud and kind of realized some things about myself. Not everyone in town has been terrible. I've got to meet some pretty great people too."

"Really? Who are these great people you've met? Would I happen to know them?" Grant wagged his eyebrows at her.

Mercedes blushed and was saved from answering by Sonja and an athletic-looking, dark-haired man.

"Mercedes, I'm sorry I did not introduce myself yesterday. I'm so glad you're here tonight. I'm Sonja Rossi, and this is my husband, Derek."

"Nice to meet you," Derek said politely. He then tried to steer his wife to the back of the church.

"No way, Derek! You know I like to sit in the front." Sonja resisted. She turned around and called out to Mercedes. "Come sit with us!"

Grateful she wouldn't have to sit by herself, Mercedes turned to Grant. "I guess I am going to sit with Sonja," she said.

Grant nodded. "Okay, but I still want to hear about these great people later."

Mercedes rolled her eyes at him and went to sit with the Rossis.

Sonja was one of those people who could carry on a conversation without effort from the other person. She told Mercedes her whole life story in about three minutes, only needing an occasional yes or no response. Sonja hailed from Hot Springs, but Derek had lived his whole life in Shady Springs, minus the time away in trade school.

"In fact," Sonja stated proudly, "Derek is the descendant from one of the early founders of Shady Springs. The Rostellers traveled with Pastor Hart to Shady Springs. They later shortened their last name to Rossi."

Derek interjected, "Mercedes doesn't want to hear our whole life story. She's really interested in genealogy." He tried to apologize for his wife's rambling.

"That's alright," Mercedes said excitedly. "I remember reading about the Rostellers in Pastor Hart's diary. It's super cool to meet someone whose relation is mentioned in the journal."

Sonja's eyes widened. "There's a diary?" Sonja turned to Derek and asked, "Did you know there was a diary?"

Derek opened his mouth to respond just as Pastor Grant stepped to the podium and welcomed everyone for coming.

It was kind of surreal for Mercedes being in a church service. They sang some hymns and some new songs. Mercedes tried to keep herself from going into critique mode. The service wasn't happening to please her or what she thought it should be; it was about simply worshiping God in humility and adoration. If the song leader sang a little off-key or the keyboardist hit a wrong note, that was their service they were bringing before God. Who was she to deem them unworthy of worship?

Grant stood to preach, and Mercedes listened awestruck. Grant didn't play around when it came to preaching. He wasn't a "screamer preacher," but he was passionate. Mercedes found herself drawn into his message. She turned to the passage out of Deuteronomy 7:17–18 (KJV), where Grant preached from.

"If thou shalt say in thine heart, These nations are more than I; how can I dispossess them? Thou shalt not be afraid of them: but shalt well remember what the LORD thy God did unto Pharaoh, and unto all Egypt." Grant continued, "When we're faced with difficulties and wonder how we can succeed or even survive, God tells us to let go of our fear and remember Him. Fear holds us back from God's blessings because fear keeps us from walking by faith."

Mercedes began to think about all that fear had kept her from. Yes, she blocked people out from hurting her, but how many people had she blocked from blessing her? Fear kept her away from hurt, but it also kept God from working in her life.

When Grant called for the invitation, Mercedes sat still. *I am not going up to the altar and making a spectacle of myself,* she resolved inwardly and grabbed the pew as an anchor.

Out of the corner of her eye, she saw Sonja slip out and pray at the altar. Then, a few more people went forward.

Just go, kneel, and pray. You can do this. Stop being afraid. Mercedes felt the Lord continue to urge her for obedience as she gripped the pew tighter.

Step out. I'm here waiting. Take the first step.

Mercedes closed her eyes and breathed out. Not making eye contact with anyone, she felt herself walking to the altar. As she knelt down, the burden and weight of everything lifted from her shoulders, and she finally felt peace. "God, I'm so sorry for pushing you away. Everything is spiraling out of control. I don't want to live my life without you. Please, lead me to the right job and place. Help me to let go of the fear that has been holding me back and to trust You. Thank you, Lord, for leading me here and for not giving up on me." Mercedes gave Sonja a small smile as she slid back into their pew.

As Grant closed the invitation and reminded them of the volleyball game after church, Mercedes realized she wasn't wearing appropriate clothes to play in. *I'll just run back to the inn and make a quick change,* she thought. Grant mentioned they had to set up the net, so it would be a while before they started. Mercedes told Sonja where she was going in case Grant asked about her and ran out to her car. As she got in her car, the wind began to whip her hair in her face, and the atmosphere felt cooler. *Might be a short game anyway, if we even get to play.*

When Mercedes got to the B&B, Bertie sat again at the tea table. Mercedes said a quick hello and ran upstairs and changed. As she started to run back out the door, Bertie called to her. Mercedes sighed and walked over to where she sat.

"I wanted you to try this new tea. I received it in the mail today. I think you will like it," Bertie said.

"I'm really in a hurry, Bertie. How about in the morning?" Mercedes asked as she turned toward the door.

Bertie's voice broke. "I made it special for you. Please, try it?"

Not wanting to upset her further, she picked up the teacup in front of her and took a drink. The tea tasted very sweet, almost like syrup. "Bertie, this is really sweet. What kind did you say it was?" Mercedes took another sip as a bitter metallic undernote hit her taste buds. "Where did this package of tea come from? I think we should check the expiration date." Mercedes put her teacup down on the table.

Bertie didn't answer her and watched her intently.

"What is it? What's wrong?" Mercedes said cautiously. She turned around to see if something or someone stood behind her. The turning movement made her very dizzy. The thunder clapped, and the lights flickered off inside the inn. "Bertie!" Mercedes called out. She closed her eyes, trying to steady herself. Her knees began to buckle as she tried to brace herself for impact before darkness finally overtook her.

11

GRANT

Time after time flashed through my mind of every instance that God's grace has helped me through. The words echoed in my heart, 'I am enough,' and I knew in that moment that He was enough.

—*Pastor Hart*

Grant Ford watched Mercedes make a hasty exit from the church, and his heart dropped. While he preached, he noticed she would nod her head in agreement occasionally and seemed to be listening intently. He was delighted when she moved forward in the invitation to pray. So, why the sudden exit? He didn't even get a chance to say goodbye. Grant started to head in her direction.

"Pastor Grant, where's the volleyball net?" Wendell and a few other youths blocked his way.

As he handed them the keys to the storage closet, he noticed Sonja and Derek leaving. "Y'all aren't going to be able to play tonight?" Grant asked.

"We're playing," Sonja assured him. "I have to get my clothes out of the car, and Derek is going to run home and get his tennis shoes."

"Yeah, I don't know why I didn't grab them," Derek said.

"Mercedes is coming as well. She had to go back to the B&B to change clothes," Sonja explained.

Grant breathed a sigh of relief. Mercedes was coming back, yet as Grant watched Derek and Sonja leave, he sensed that something wasn't quite right.

Derek Rossi couldn't believe it when his wife asked Mercedes Lewis to sit with them at church. Then, as if that wasn't enough, she started telling Mercedes about his family history. Derek watched Mercedes' reaction very carefully after Sonja blabbed about his family. Mercedes didn't give away any facial expression or body language indicating that she had read about his dark family secret. Perhaps she had read it and didn't think it as horrible as his family had thought all these years.

Sonja was extremely proud of her family heritage. Her family came from a famous Spanish conquistador, whose name Derek couldn't pronounce. When she decided to research Derek's family history, she was elated to see his family name along with the town's founding fathers. Derek felt bad lying to his wife. He knew if he wanted his marriage to survive, he would have to do something to finish this once and for all. He went home and grabbed the journal from where he stashed it. Derek had hidden it under the guest bedroom's mattress. Not very original, but still effective. He carefully unwrapped the leather binding around it and opened it up to the passage he had read the day before.

Monday, March 3, 1856

Today, my family has faced devastation beyond repair. Lois Rosteller came to my house in an uproar. Mary said that he was drunk and waving his pocket revolver around. I left to help one of the men in our church repair the roof on his house that had been damaged in a storm. Glennis was home with Mary and Edwin. Apparently, Sarah and Emily left again, and Lois thought they were taking refuge at our house like they usually do.

Mary said her mother talked Lois down from his rage, and he apologized profusely and laid his gun down on the table. He began sobbing, and Glennis fixed him some coffee to help sober him up. Edwin then entered our home, heedless of the happenings going on, saw the revolver on the table, and picked it up. The gun went off. And my beautiful wife, my one true companion, was shot in the stomach. It . . . I . . . I don't know what I am feeling. Horror and sorrow for my children witnessing the death of their mother. Anguish and grief for the loss of my wife. Anger at Lois Rosteller for bringing the blasted gun into my home. In my mind, I know it was no one's fault. Lois didn't purposely set out to murder my wife. And my poor son, I don't know how he will get through all of this without being overcome with guilt.

In my heart, though, I blame Lois, and honestly, a little to my son. He's old enough now to know how serious guns are. Why did he pick it up? Why did Lois even bring it? And then my heart whispers, Why did God let this happen? I'm not supposed to ask why, though. Right? I'm the preacher, the man of God. I must tell myself all the things I tell others in their time of grief. My wife is in a better place. I will see her again someday. God will work this out for good. However, our hurt is still there, and the trauma still lingers on. The sheriff came, and after I told him what really happened, I requested there not to be a report made. I could not bear my son to go through town with people blaming him, and I wanted to keep Lois out of it as well. The blame and guilt the townspeople would have placed on Lois would have sent him over the edge. I hope he can get it together for Mary and Emily's sake if they give him another chance.

After the children went to sleep, I came and just sat out by the lake. The sun came up. A new day was starting to a new life that I didn't know how to live. How do I do this, Lord? How do I raise my children without their mother? How do I pastor a church without my wife? I cried, and I searched the sky, and I saw the cloud. I remembered how God led my family and protected us all these years, through cholera, through traveling in a wilderness, through a miscarriage we had before Edwin was born. Time after time flashed through my mind of every instance that God's grace has helped me through. The words echoed in my heart, "I am enough," and I knew at that moment that He was enough.

I threw myself to my knees, and I thanked the Lord for everything He had done for me, for sending me Glennis and my children. By the time I finished praying, I knew we would overcome this travesty.

Friday, March 7, 1856

We had Glennis's service the day before yesterday. She looked beautiful in her favorite blue dress. Mary sang one of her favorite hymns. Edwin wrote a poem to honor her. I am so proud of my children and how they have come through this period of grief. I know that we still have a long way ahead of us. I've been watching Edwin carefully, and he seems to be doing okay. He broke down Thursday and asked me if I hated him. Of course, I assured him that I loved him and would always love him. I couldn't fathom how he could think any other feeling would be possible and came to the conclusion that I need to be more attentive to expressing my feelings. Glennis was always better at that than me.

We heard back from Sarah and Emily. They had traveled to Hot Springs to stay with Sarah's parents. Sarah sent her condolences but did not return for the funeral. She didn't want to face Lois and wrote she may not ever come back.

Last night, I went to talk to Lois. He was in a bad place at the funeral. The guilt he bore completely shrouded his countenance. Most of the townspeople assumed it was from losing his family, but of course, I know different.

Sarah convinced Lois to move to Shady Springs about four years ago as an ultimatum. The men in our congregation helped them build their cabin. As a couple, Lois and Sarah seemed like they had been doing better. They seemed happy up until this last year. Lois hurt himself working in a manganese mine in January and had been home for three months. Sarah hadn't mentioned to anyone that he had started drinking again or was headed in a downward spiral.

When I went to check on him, Lois sat alone inside his cabin in the dark. The smell of despondency and alcohol hung intertwined in the air. He asked me if I was there to kill him. Truth be told, I think part of him wanted me to. When I told him I simply wanted to check on him, he asked me why. I told him the Lord loved Lois Rosteller, and I was supposed to show His love to others.

Lois sat there a minute and processed what I said. "Sorry, Pastor," he told me, "I'm not buying into God's love anymore." He beheld me with red-rimmed eyes and a glazed expression and walked out the front door. I stood to follow him out. He ignored me completely and walked out to his barn. I decided there wasn't much left to say, not at least until he sobered up. I mounted my horse and hollered out to him that

I would be back again tomorrow. A gunshot stilled the air. I don't really know what happened next. I ran to the barn, and there his body lay in a puddle of blood on the ground.

Somehow, I got to town and relayed to the sheriff all of the events that transpired. The sheriff stared at me kind of strange. He saddled up his horse and followed me back out to the barn. On the ride back, it dawned on me what the sheriff might be thinking. He must have thought I killed Lois out of retribution for my wife's death. Blessedly, after the sheriff saw the body, he told me he knew that the gunshot had been self-inflicted. This did little to ease my mind over the shock and guilt I felt. No, I did not pull the trigger on Lois Rosteller, but I was his pastor. How could I have missed what his intentions were?

Derek had a feeling that Sarah Rosteller changed her name to Sarah Rossi to be rid of the tarnished name. His father had told him that their last name was changed because people would always misspell it.

Looked like drinking ran in his family as well. Derek, himself, had never tasted a drop because his father had been such an idiot about liquor. His father had never been violent; he just hadn't been present in Derek's life. Derek Sr. wouldn't have known if his son attended class at school, much less his grade level. Derek knew that he would not have made it in this life if it wasn't for his church.

As a child, he rode the bus to church on Sundays merely to get away from his father. Chase had been his Sunday school teacher back then and always checked in with him on Saturdays to see if he was going to attend. He hung out with the youth group, and when the opportunity came to leave for trade school, he took it faster than a sneeze through a screen door. The day he met Sonja, his black-and-white world turned to technicolor. He loved her vibrant outlook on life. Every day seemed an adventure; Sonja was fearless. Derek was amazed and humbled to be loved by her.

"God, I know I haven't talked to You much, but please let her still love me despite all I've done. Please help her realize I am not my past. And, God, if for some reason she doesn't, help me not to lose it. Can you show me a life in You?" Derek grabbed the journal and went back to the church.

Grant was relieved when Derek appeared, even though he kept watching for Mercedes. The teens were crushing the adults. The wind started picking up, and it seemed like the storm that had been on the verge was about to make its appearance.

"Dude, I am so glad you're here," Grant said as Derek got on the court.

"Yeah," one of the teens cried out, "Maybe y'all will be able to serve it over the net now."

"Less trash talk, more volley!" Grant retorted as he tossed Derek the volleyball. "Your serve!" he called as he went to the net.

"You got this, babe!" Sonja encouragingly called out on his left.

Derek threw the ball up and slammed it over to the other side. Two teenage girls squealed and ran out of the way. With Derek on their side, the adults made a good comeback and ended up winning.

Grant felt concerned Mercedes never made it back to the church. He didn't receive any messages from her, and he wondered if there was a problem with her news story or something. He tried calling her, but it went straight to voicemail. Grant went over to Gertie, who was helping the older ladies serve pizza to the kids after the game. But she hadn't heard from Mercedes either. Grant couldn't shake the feeling that something was wrong. He decided he would go and check on Mercedes to make sure she was safe. He made his way toward his truck when Derek and Sonja appeared.

"Pastor Grant, do you have time to talk? It's important." Derek asked.

Grant knew he couldn't put Derek off, especially since Derek was the one initiating the conversation. Grant sent Gertie a quick text saying he had a meeting and if she heard from Mercedes to text him. "Sure," Grant said as he put on a smile, "let's go sit in my office."

On the way back to his office, Sonja kept glancing at Derek in puzzlement. When they finally sat down, Derek began to speak. "Sonja doesn't really know why we're here, Pastor Grant. I figured it would be easier to get this out once and for all."

Grant wasn't surprised when Derek admitted he took the journal after he snooped around in Grant's office. He had seemed the most obvious culprit. Grant almost laughed out loud as Derek confessed to lying about missing their appointment because he thought the sheriff was there to arrest him. When Derek finished his tale, he apologized for everything again and handed the journal back to Grant.

Sonja was more upset with Derek for thinking that she would break up their marriage over something that happened over 100 years ago. "I married you, Derek, not your distant great-great-grandfather! You're not a drunk, you are not your father, and I love you," Sonja said as she squeezed his knee. "Although, you are going to have to make this up to me for not being truthful."

Derek groaned. "Look, I'm saved, but I didn't grow up in a Christian home. I'm not sure what a Christian home even looks like. I know you grew up in a good home with good parents, and I want that for us. I'm just not comfortable with talking about God and praying with people. It's not that I don't want to; it's just something I'm not used to."

Sonja reached over and took his hand. "Derek, the fact that you are willing to and truly want to makes all the difference to me."

"We have an idea of a perfect family in our mind, but the truth is we can only be made perfect in Christ. Having a relationship with Christ and building upon that personal relationship with Him is what is going to make your marriage even stronger," Grant interjected.

"I think that's where I need to start—my relationship with God." Derek glanced at Sonja, who squeezed his hand assuredly.

"That is a great place to start," Grant said as his phone began ringing. He checked the caller ID and saw Gertie's name flash on the screen. Immediately, Grant knew something was wrong. "I'm sorry. I really need to take this. If you want, we can set up another time to talk?"

Derek and Sonja nodded and thanked him.

Grant answered the phone as they left his office.

Before he could say hello, Gertie began to cry hysterically. "Pastor Grant, you have to come quick. It's Mercedes. Something awful has happened!"

As he got into his truck, thunder cracked, and hail began to bounce off his windshield. He was thankful all his parishioners had left for the safety of their homes.

Shady Spring's beloved cloud was enveloped by dark navy and gray storm clouds pulsing with lights as if they were in a light show. Five bolts of lightning pierced through the clouds, zapping the lake as if they were the very fingers of God.

Grant had never seen a storm like this one. "God, You are controlling this light show. Give us safety in this storm. Let me get to Mercedes safely and quickly." He wondered what had happened. Did her tormentor somehow get to her? Had there been an accident? He tried to pray but couldn't think of the words to say. "God, please let her be alright. I know you brought her into this town, into my life for a reason. She's one of Your children. Please, let her be okay."

As he pulled into the B&B, he heard the wail of an ambulance drawing nearer.

12

MERCEDES

Everything will all work out, and something good will come out of this. The Bible promises us that.

—Janet Lewis

My head feels as if it has been rammed into a wall, Mercedes thought. She heard a faint beeping sound coming from somewhere in the darkness. *Oh, Lord. What happened to me?*

She tried to open her eyes, but they were so heavy, like bags of sand were weighing them down. She tried to remember the last thing she did. She was at the inn. She changed her clothes and went to go play volleyball. Wait, no, she stopped to talk to Bertie, and Bertie gave her some tea. The tea tasted sweet and weird. Bertie acted oddly, too, almost maniacal, then everything went black. Mercedes heard a moaning sound, then realized it was her. She was the one moaning. Then, she heard someone call out her name.

"Mercedes."

The voice she heard sounded so far away.

"Mercedes, can you hear me?"

The voice sounded closer. Mercedes wanted to open her eyes, to answer back, but a heavy blanket of darkness enveloped her. All of a sudden, a small pinhole of light shone through her lashes and grew bigger and bigger until her eyes opened fully. The bright light faded to muted colors around the room as she began to focus on her surroundings.

Grant sat in a chair beside her bed, studying her intently. His piercing brown eyes filled with concern. "Grant," she whispered. Her throat was so parched and hoarse as she held out her hand to him. He reached over and gently took her hand.

"I hoped you'd wake up while I was here. How are you feeling?"

"My head hurts, and my throat is so dry. What happened to me?"

Grant carefully let go of her hand and pushed the nurse button. "I'm calling the nurse to bring you some water. When Gertie came home from church last night, you were lying on the floor unconscious. She immediately called me and then called 9-1-1. I got there right before the ambulance arrived. Your head was bleeding, and you were unresponsive. Bertie kept spewing nonsense about getting rid of the evil so the cloud would stay."

"Bertie gave me some tea. There must have been something in it."

"There sure was, honey," replied the nurse as she came bustling in. "My name is Lateka, and I am going to be your nurse today. It's a wonder you're awake already. You were given quite a cocktail of codeine and NyQuil™. We weren't sure how many she gave you, so we had to pump your stomach, which is why your throat hurts like Hades." Lateka pushed a button to help Mercedes sit upright as she handed her a cup of ice chips.

"Thank you," Mercedes said.

Lateka checked Mercedes' stats and made notes on her chart. "The doctor will be in later to see you. We got everything out of your system, though, and there shouldn't be any long-term effects."

"Long-term effects?" Grant asked.

"A lot of times in cases of an overdose, there are injuries to the brain, heart, lung, and kidneys. You're quite blessed to come through with minimal injury," Lateka answered as she left the room.

"I am blessed," Mercedes whispered in agreement. She glanced over at Grant. He had huge circles under his eyes, and his clothes were wrinkled. "Were you here all night?"

"Yes, I didn't want you to wake up and be alone. Your mom is on her way here. She should be here any minute now." He sheepishly ran his fingers through his hair.

Mercedes closed her eyes. *My mom is totally going to freak out.* "Thanks, Grant." She placed her hand over his hand. "It was so nice of you to stay even though we haven't known each other very long."

Grant put his other hand on top of her hand and gently squeezed it.

Mercedes yawned. "Grant," she whispered. She wanted to tell him so much, but her eyelids were getting heavier, and her thoughts were swimming through a thick fog.

"Yes?" Grant said.

"I think I like you." Mercedes drifted back to sleep with a smile.

The next time Mercedes woke, a thin, middle-aged woman sat in the chair Grant previously occupied. "Mom?" Mercedes thought she remembered Grant said her mom was coming, but she didn't know if she was hallucinating.

"Mercedes! You're awake!" Her mom hovered over her with relief. Janet Lewis smoothed her daughter's forehead and gently kissed her.

"I'm so glad you're here. So many things have happened." Mercedes felt tears well in her eyes.

"Are you okay? Do you want me to call the nurse?" Janet handed her some tissue.

"No, you don't need to call. I just feel sore."

Janet assured her, "The doctor came by and said that you would feel that way. He also mentioned that you could probably go home tomorrow."

"Good. Did Grant go home?"

Janet replied with a twinkle in her eye. "Yes. I sent him home. Poor thing looked exhausted. He didn't really want to leave you, but I think he knew better than to argue with your mother."

Mercedes couldn't help but smile at the thought of her mom telling Grant what to do.

"Aha, I knew it! You do like him. I can tell!" Janet said triumphantly.

"Mom!" Mercedes tried to scold her, but it came out in a deep voice because of her throat. The deep voice made them both laugh, which made Mercedes' throat hurt even more. "OW!" she grabbed her throat.

"Oh, hon, I'm sorry!" Her mom handed her the cup of ice chips as Lateka came back into the room.

"Seems like we are feeling somewhat better in here! Mommas make the best nurses." Lateka winked at Mercedes as she checked her vitals.

"They really do," Mercedes agreed.

"I see Pastor Grant left. Never seen him worry over someone so much before," Lateka said.

Mercedes felt her face getting hot.

"You know, I see him occasionally check in on his church members and come to counsel people. I always recognize him by his mustache and his motorcycle. Everybody in town's been dying to see who he would settle down for." Lateka winked at Mercedes.

"Oh, we aren't really, well, we just met really . . ." Mercedes stopped trying to explain and threw some more ice chips in her mouth. "Throat hurts," she said, pointing to her throat while her mom and Lateka grinned.

Lateka gave Mercedes some lozenges and told her she would be back later to check in on her.

As she left, Gertie came and stood in the doorway. "May I come in?"

"Of course, Gertie," Mercedes answered.

"Mom, this is Gertie. She runs the B&B where I am staying." Mercedes tilted her head toward Gertie. "What happened with Bertie? Why did she do this to me?"

"Wait a minute. Who is Bertie? You know who did this to my daughter?" Janet demanded. She walked a few steps toward Gertie, and her face began to turn red.

"Mom, calm down. Bertie is Gertie's sister. She has dementia. Let her explain," Mercedes said.

Gertie began, "Before I explain, let me just say how sorry I am. I didn't realize how far Bertie's illness had accelerated. This morning, I found emails asking you to investigate our cloud on Bertie's computer. I thought all she did on that thing was play solitaire. I couldn't have been more wrong."

"I guess that makes sense. We thought the person who wrote the emails was older. But why did she reach out to me?" Mercedes asked.

Gertie bowed her head. "This whole thing is my fault. Apparently, while we were watching you on the news one day, I commented that you resembled Bertie when she was younger. Bertie said that was the moment she knew you had to be her daughter."

"What?" Mercedes and her mom said simultaneously.

"Bertie got it in her head that she didn't really lose her baby. In her mind, the baby survived, and our father lied and gave the baby away for adoption. I know it doesn't make a lot of sense. You are too young to be her daughter, but that's what was in her mind."

"Wait a minute. Why did Bertie try to kill me then if she thought I was her daughter?"

"At first, Bertie thought that you could help with sustaining the cloud. When she saw the cloud still deteriorating, Bertie decided that you were evil, and she would help the town by getting rid of you. She placed notes in your room, trying to scare you away, but she grew more desperate as the cloud kept shrinking. So, she waited for you at the hotel and tried to drug you." Gertie began to cry. "I'm so sorry, Mercedes. I planned on moving her into a nursing facility before all of this occurred. That is why I met with Pastor Grant the other day. I'm too old to give her the type of care that she needs. She spent the night in jail. They arrested her for attempted murder. I think they are supposed to give her some sort of capacity test. I don't know what they are going to do with her. I went to visit her this morning, and she was so confused. She didn't even remember anything from yesterday."

Mercedes felt an ache in her heart for Gertie. "It's alright, Gertie. You couldn't have known," Mercedes said. Janet handed some tissue to Gertie while wiping some tears from her own eyes. "I'll do what I can to help her. Surely, they won't go to trial over this. What a mess."

Gertie's face paled as two police officers came into the room.

"Excuse us. Mercedes Lewis?" one of the uniformed officers spoke, giving Mercedes a questioning look.

"Yes, that's me," Mercedes said.

"We have a few questions about last night and need to get your statement."

Mercedes was about to answer them when her mother interrupted.

"My daughter just woke up and is in a lot of pain. Can't this wait until tomorrow?"

"Mom, it's okay. We want to leave tomorrow, remember?" Mercedes didn't want to have to be in the hospital longer than she had to.

Gertie backed out of the hospital room while nervously eyeing the detectives. "I'm going to head home, Mercedes. Call me if you need anything. Janet, we have room at the inn if you need a place to stay tonight."

After Gertie left, Mercedes told the officers everything she remembered about the night before. She also asked if the state would prosecute Bertie if she didn't want to press charges. Her heart sank when the officers explained the crime committed was a felony and there would be charges against Bertie. If Bertie failed the capacity test, she would be sent to a hospital where she could get help.

The officers left behind a somber atmosphere. Mercedes finally broke the silence. "Mom, I don't understand it. I feel like I got everything right with God, and then this happened."

Janet squeezed her daughter's hand. "What do you mean?"

Mercedes felt a tear roll down her cheek. "I mean, since I've been away at college and started my career, I left God on the sidelines. I never got over what happened at our church with Garrett and with the music minister. I felt so hurt and angry. Then, those feelings turned to bitterness." Mercedes glanced at her mom, expecting to see judgment and was touched to see tears in her mother's eyes.

Her mom confessed, "I knew you were hurting. Your dad and I hated the fact that those events hindered your walk with God. We were so afraid you would turn your back on God completely. It was hard for us not to get bitter with those people at church. But we went to them, and we forgave them. We've all been praying so hard for God to keep you safe and that you would one day come back to Him."

Can you see Me working now? A small voice imprinted on her heart.

Mercedes couldn't help as more tears fell. "But, Mom, I did. I did come back to Him. I told Him I wanted His will for my life, and then this happened. Look where I am. I'm in a hospital!"

Janet gave Mercedes a no-nonsense look. "That's right. You are in a hospital, but you are alive, Mercedes. You could be dead, but God allowed you to live. You could be injured permanently, but God allowed your injuries to be temporary. God is working in your life, Mercedes Lewis. Don't they say there's a silver lining in every cloud?"

Mercedes laughed as she cried. *Okay, God, I get it. I see You, I hear You. Thank You for being patient with me.* "I know, Mom, you're right. I guess I was feeling a little sorry for myself."

Janet patted her hand. "It's okay, hon. We all feel sorry for ourselves at times, but we can't wallow in it. Everything will all work out, and something good will come out of this. The Bible promises us that."

As if on cue, Grant walked in carrying two milk-shakes. "Hello, ladies! I brought a little something to help with your throat." He handed Mercedes her milkshake with a spoon and the other one to her mom.

Her mother gushed, "Thank you, Grant. You didn't get one for yourself?"

Mercedes answered for him. "No, Mom. Grant doesn't eat sugar."

Her mother looked at him funny. "Are you diabetic or something?"

Mercedes rolled her eyes as she dipped her spoon in her shake. "Mom, no. He likes healthy stuff, for some weird reason." Mercedes winked at Grant and grinned. "Seriously, though, thank you for the shake. This is just what I needed."

As Mercedes relished her ice cream, she listened to her mom and Grant talk. Her mom asked him where he was from and about his family. *Oh my gosh, she's going to ask him his whole life story if I don't stop her!* "Mom, give him a break. Are you going to write a biography about the man?"

Janet raised her hands in defense. "I'm simply trying to get to know him. After all, he did watch over you until I could get here."

"It's fine," Grant said modestly. "I do have something else to share with you, though." He pulled out the familiar leather journal out of his jacket.

13

MERCEDES

Then shall we know, if we follow on to know the LORD . . .

—Hosea 6:3 (KJV)

Her heart skipped a beat at the sight of the journal. "You found it!" Mercedes exclaimed. "Oh my goodness, where was it? Mom, this is the journal from the town's founding pastor, Judd Hart."

"Well, somebody did end up taking it, but they returned it after they realized the error of their ways," Grant said.

"I'm glad they returned it, although it would have been nice to have for the news story. Did you read any further into it?" Mercedes asked.

"No, I haven't. Would you like me to read the rest to you?"

Mercedes and her mother both said they would like that.

"Before you start, is the cloud still here?" Mercedes asked.

"Too many storm clouds to tell," Grant replied as he sat down to read.

Mercedes cleared her throat and said, "This cloud has meant different things to the townspeople of Shady Springs throughout the years. I know some people think the cloud leaving is because of disapproval from God. But maybe it's because what you are doing is right? Maybe God sees the people in Shady Springs are faithful, and they are ready for that next step in their journey of faith. They are finally ready to walk by faith and not by sight."

"Can you repeat that again?" Grant said. "I want to write it down for Sunday's sermon."

Mercedes and her mom laughed.

"It is true, though, when you think back to the children of Israel. They had to practice their faith for forty years in the wilderness until they were ready for their next step of faith."

Mercedes wondered what her next step of faith would be. She had so many things left up in the air. A few days prior, she was terrified. Now, Mercedes felt anticipation. She knew that God really did have something for her and quite possibly someone for her as well.

Grant picked up reading where they had left off. Mercedes was stunned when he read how Glennis died and the circumstances surrounding her death. She teared up when he read about the funeral and Lois Rosteller's suicide. He finally read the last journal entry.

A WISP OF FAITH

Tuesday, March 3, 1857

Today marks the one-year anniversary of my wife's death. This year has been extremely hard—the holidays especially. Reflecting back through the years, I realized how much I took her for granted. I have no idea how she did it all. Glennis loved caring for the other women in our congregation. She always had time for ministry, along with everything else she did. Mary and Edwin have had to grow up a lot this past year, more than I would have preferred them to. They help with dinner and tidying the house.

There has been a lot of speculation from townspeople (mostly non-parishioners) about Lois Rosteller's death and my being there when he died. Most of it has died down now, but I feel his death shadows me still. I still feel guilty about not being able to stop him from ending his life. Sarah and Emily have moved back into town, and I find myself trying to make it up to them by fixing things on their homestead.

Through everything, we still have our cloud floating over the lake. I used to gaze upon it and shamefully wonder what would have happened if we had just gone and settled in Cedar Ridge or even if we had never left Haven at all. Would my Glennis still be here? In answer to my inquiry, the Lord sent flashbacks of memories to remind me of all His work that we accomplished here in Shady Springs and the precious souls won here by both myself and Glennis. Then, the Lord gently reminds me that Glennis is

His, and what a blessing it was that I had her the time that I did. Now, when I look upon the cloud, I remember Glennis's faith and our journey together following the Lord, and I think upon my life verse. "Then shall we know, if we follow on to know the LORD . . ." Hosea 6:3 (KJV).

Grant closed the journal carefully. "I guess that's it," he said. "I'm probably going to have to turn this over to the historical society or something. I wanted to read it first, though." He glanced at Mercedes. He was curious to know her thoughts, especially since, at first, she seemed a little closed off to things concerning God. "So, what do you think now? In the beginning, you were sort of incredulous about God leading people nowadays through a cloud."

Mercedes set her ice cream down. "At first, I had my doubts," she admitted. "But now, I believe God used that cloud to guide them. As to why God has left the cloud here for so long? I don't know. I guess He has still been using it to lead people. I mean, He brought me here to Shady Springs."

To you, a voice interjected in Grant's head. *I brought her here to you.* Not quite sure what to do with that information, Grant tried to focus again on what Mercedes was saying.

"I would never have come here if the cloud hadn't been here," Mercedes added as she finished her milkshake. "Could one of y'all open up the window blinds?" Mercedes asked. "I think the sun is starting to come out."

Grant went over to the window and lifted the blinds. The thought that Mercedes was here for him was overwhelming. *Am I ready to move on? To love again? Am I willing to miss out on God's plan for my life because of my own fear?* He pushed his questions and feelings aside to sort out later. "Wow!" Grant exclaimed. "Now, this is a room with a view!" He wasn't kidding either. The hospital room had an excellent view of the lake. Their little cloud, which overshadowed the lake, was replaced with something that Grant had never seen before. Several large, long clouds stretched from east to west like giant white ropes rolling across the bright blue sky.

"Oh, my gosh!" Mercedes said, "I can't believe this. I've always wanted to see one of these." She pushed her arms against the rails and swung her feet off the hospital bed.

"What are you doing, Mercedes? You can't just get up and go. You're in a hospital gown!" her mom reminded her, tipping her head in Grant's direction. Mercedes paid her mother no mind as she took off her monitors.

Grant didn't know what to do. Should he get a nurse? "What are you trying to do?" Grant asked hesitantly.

"I've got to get outside and see this cloud," Mercedes said, crossing her arms. "It won't last long. There have been sightings in Oklahoma and Iowa, but I don't think they've ever seen one here in Arkansas."

Mercedes grabbed her hospital blanket and wrapped it around her so she was decently covered. With a determined gleam in her eye, she tried to stand and walk but almost fell over with her wobbly legs.

"Mercedes, wait. We can call for a wheelchair," her mother pleaded. Janet looked over at Grant for support.

"It will be too late, Mom. I'm going to miss it!" Mercedes said.

Without even thinking, Grant walked over and scooped Mercedes up in her blanket cocoon and started carrying her out of the room. "Come on, then. Let's go see this cloud before we get caught by the orderly!" he said.

"Grant!" Janet gasped in shock as he carried her daughter down the hall.

"Mom, grab my phone, please, so I can take pictures," Mercedes called over his shoulder. "Thanks, Grant. I owe you big for this," Mercedes said excitedly.

"Pastor Ford, where are you taking our patient?" Lateka stood with her arms crossed, blocking their way.

"She's just getting some fresh air," Grant replied. "We'll be back in the room in a jiffy. You better move. I don't want to drop her."

Lateka moved aside quickly, shaking her head.

"Are you sure you've got me?" Mercedes tightened her grip around his neck.

"Absolutely," Grant assured her, even though his arms were starting to burn. He prayed he didn't drop her.

They made it outside in time to see the clouds roll through.

"They're called Morning Glory clouds," Mercedes whispered close to his ear. "Aren't they magnificent?"

Grant stood speechless. He was too occupied watching her instead of the clouds. The sunlight radiated on Mercedes in her simple hospital gown and sheet with an almost halo effect. Grant had a sudden glimpse of what his future could be—of him carrying her in her wedding dress. The magnitude of this revelation shocked him to his core, and his eyes began to mist.

He blinked a couple of times, hoping Mercedes wouldn't notice, and tried desperately to focus on the clouds. They truly were magnificent. The clouds were rope-like and puffy. It was as if God took three cotton balls and pulled and twisted them, stretching them across His brilliant blue sky. The clouds appeared like they were rolling backward as they were moving forward.

It was one of the most amazing things Grant had ever seen. He turned his head toward Mercedes to tell her something. At the exact time, she leaned in to whisper something to him, resulting in her lips brushing against his nose. Her lips were still cold from the milkshake. Grant felt a shiver run down his spine.

Mercedes' face turned red in less than two seconds, and she began to apologize. "I'm so sorry, Grant. That was totally an accident."

Grant grinned. "We need to work on your aim. You were a little off."

"Grant!" Mercedes' eyes widened.

"What?" Grant said innocently. "Would you like to try again?"

Lateka came out behind them with a wheelchair. "Please, no. Don't try this again. I thought if your brief insane moment of chivalry had passed, Mercedes could use the wheelchair." She rolled her eyes at Grant.

Grant gingerly placed Mercedes in the chair.

Janet slyly looked at Mercedes as she handed the phone to her daughter to take pictures. When Janet saw him raise his eyebrows at her in question, she smiled. "I took a few pictures myself."

As they literally watched the clouds roll away, there remained an empty blue sky except for a couple of cranes gracefully soaring by. A peace existed on the lake that only happens after the throes of a storm have passed.

Grant knew he would remember this moment forever.

"Well, that's it." Mercedes sighed. "The cloud is gone."

Grant heard a ping from his phone. It was a text from Grumpy Old Men, Grant, Harold, and Chase's text group. Grant came up with the name as a joke, and Harold and Chase thought it hilarious. Unfortunately, the text received was not as funny.

Elders want to meet at the church. It's not looking good.

Grant's heart sank as he responded, *Alright, be there soon. It's in God's hands.*

"What's wrong?" Mercedes asked, noticing his solemn expression.

"The town elders want to meet," Grant replied, trying to remain calm.

Mercedes frowned. "Are they really going to ask you to leave over this cloud?"

Grant nodded. "It appears so. It'll be alright. I've called some preacher friends of mine for advice. God sometimes calls us to different places for different seasons. I've got to meet with the elders now. I'll come by later to check on you."

"Alright." Mercedes ducked her head a little and smiled. She gazed up at him, and the sun hit her eyes so that they sparkled amber and green. *Literally breathtaking.*

"Well, okay, we'll see you later then," Janet said, shaking her head and laughing, interrupting the awkward pause.

Mercedes waved to Grant as Lateka started to wheel her back inside the hospital.

Grant walked to his motorcycle with a million thoughts racing through his mind. He supposed riding up to the church on his motorcycle would only fuel the council's decision to get rid of him. *Too late to change my ride now, though.*

When he arrived at the church, Chase and Harold were there with tears in their eyes. The elders hadn't arrived yet.

"It's not right. I've spent all these years serving in this church, trying to show the next generations how to live by the Book. And here you are, fruit of this church's ministry, and some uppity, white-walled . . ." Chase's voice broke, and he shook his head in anger.

"It's okay, Chase." Grant tried to calm him. He didn't like Chase getting so worked up. "What time are they going to be here?" he asked Harold.

Harold shook his head. "The council isn't coming. They decided that since Chase and I have worked with you closely these past years, then we should be the ones to tell you what a bunch of idiots they are. I am so sorry, Grant."

Grant felt like he was punched in the gut. "So, when do they want me out of here?"

"The end of the month," Harold said.

"So, two weeks?" Grant was in shock. He thought he would have a bit longer to figure out where he was supposed to go.

"The council said you could still preach till then, and the church would have a fellowship on your last Sunday. They want to keep everything cordial without hurting the flock," Chase added.

Grant teared up at the mention of his flock. All the time and prayer and energy he spent on each precious soul. The teenagers and his senior saints, the new young married couples who had recently started coming—Grant had felt that they were on the verge of a new revival. Now, he was supposed to leave them? "How?" he said hoarsely. "I feel like I am abandoning my people. I won't cause a stink or throw a tantrum because I don't want them to lose the growth they've gained. But how do I do this graciously? What am I supposed to say?"

Harold put his arm on his shoulder. "You simply tell them God is leading you somewhere else and leave it at that. You love everyone, and if they need, they can always reach out to you."

Grant nodded mutely while Harold and Chase took turns hugging him. Then, they all prayed together.

As Grant watched Harold and Chase drive off the parking lot, he felt his heart break. He had depended on them for so long. He knew he had been blessed to have such godly men in his life. Leaving Shady Springs and his congregation, not to mention his family, was going to be one of the hardest things he'd done in his life. He groaned, thinking about telling his mother the news. She would insist on knowing why he was leaving and where he thought he would be going. *God,*

where am I going? Show me the way You want me to go!
And could you show me quickly, please, God, like in two
weeks? Grant prayed as he got back on his motorcycle.

When he returned to the hospital, Mercedes was
back in bed and arguing with Lateka for an early release.

"Girl, you already got me in trouble running out of
the hospital like you did," Lateka hollered back at her
as she left the room. She shook her finger in Grant's
face as he approached Mercedes' room. "You better
behave, preacher man, or you're gonna be preaching
at your funeral!"

Grant raised his eyebrows at Mercedes as he stepped
into her room. "Are you being bad?"

"Yes, I'm ready to get out of here and go home,"
Mercedes admitted.

"It won't be too much longer. You'll make it."
Grant chuckled.

Janet stood up and stretched. "I think I'm going
to go check out the snack machine."

They ignored the obvious ruse, and Grant sat in a
chair beside the hospital bed.

"So, what happened?" Mercedes asked.

Grant laid his hands in his lap. "I am looking for
a church to pastor. It's a new adventure," he said flatly.

"I'm sorry. I know it's not what you wanted. It's
not fair."

Grant leaned back in the chair. "It is what it is.
I've got some friends inquiring around to see what's
available. I know God has somewhere for me."

Mercedes brightened. "You can join my no job
club. It's pretty exclusive. Only one member right now."

Smiling, Grant replied, "What do I have to do to
join?"

"Well, seeing you brought me a milkshake and literally swept me off my feet, I think you have met the requirements. You've made quite the impression with the club president," Mercedes answered.

"Does this club have meetings that I will need to attend? Bi-monthly? Weekly? I want to keep up my membership."

"Definitely bi-monthly meetings. But if you keep impressing the president, then possibly weekly," Mercedes said.

"I think I can handle that. Consider me a member, and thank you," Grant said.

"For what?" Mercedes asked.

"For following the cloud," he answered. He lifted her soft, delicate hand to his lips and lightly kissed it.

14

MERCEDES

This was God changing the heart of man.

—Mercedes

Mercedes couldn't believe that two weeks had passed since her first trip to Shady Springs. Now, she was there again for Grant's final sermon and the church's celebratory send-off for him. She didn't understand how the church could do this to him. His congregation obviously loved him. What was the purpose of all this? Mercedes and his sister, Alice, had spent all weekend helping him pack his house and office. Grant's mom graciously offered to allow Mercedes to stay at her home while they were helping Grant pack. While hesitant to stay with them at first, Carol and Alice had practically insisted.

Mercedes took a quick liking to Alice. She had the same hair coloring as Grant, but instead of his brown eyes, Alice had light blue eyes, the same as their mother.

Alice loved her brother fiercely and struggled over the church's decision to fire him. "I don't get it. He gives everything to these people, and they don't care. They'll never have another pastor as good as my brother."

"I don't think the congregation really had a choice," Mercedes answered.

"Well, they could still do something. They just follow whatever the deacon board says."

"I've been praying for something to happen to change the board's mind," Mercedes admitted.

"Me too," Alice said.

"Me three," Grant said as he appeared in the doorway to his office.

"How long have you been eavesdropping?" Mercedes asked.

"Long enough to hear my sister say nice things about me, which I've recorded so I can replay at moments when she is mad at me." Grant laughed as Alice stuck her tongue out at him.

"I would throw something at you if we hadn't packed everything up already!"

"Yeah, I guess we are finished in here," Grant said. He gave a smile, but it didn't reach his eyes. Alice got up and hugged him. She gave her brother a serious look. "I'm hungry. Feed me."

The three of them laughed.

"What? I'm a starving college student, don't you know?" Alice shrugged her shoulders and tried to look pitiful.

"I've worked up an appetite too," Mercedes agreed, rising to her feet. "Let's go to the diner."

Grant put one arm around his sister and one arm around Mercedes. "Let's go then. Nothing worse than hangry women."

Mercedes and Alice rolled their eyes at him as they left his former office.

"I think this is our booth," Grant said as he took Mercedes' hand in his hand from across the table.

"Seriously?" Alice shook her head at her brother while Mercedes laughed.

"This is the same booth we ate at last time," she explained.

"My brother acts so weird around you," Alice said as she took a big bite of her hamburger.

"It's okay. I don't think it's weird," Mercedes smiled at Grant.

"Y'all gonna have to quit this googly eye stuff," Alice said between bites. "I'm gonna lose my appetite!"

Mercedes was about to reply when her phone rang. Her finger stretched to press the ignore button until she saw it was her old boss, Reggie, calling.

"Hello?" she answered.

"Mercedes, how are you?"

"I'm good, Reggie, and you?" Grant's eyes widened at the mention of her old boss's name.

"Great. Now, that's out of the way; the station would like to do a follow-up story on Shady Springs—sort of a 'life after the cloud' piece. Do you think you are up for it? Do you still have your connections?"

"Yes, I still have my connections." Mercedes smiled at Grant, then continued. "Actually, the Shady Springs Church is having a special service tomorrow with an old-fashioned picnic on the grounds afterward. It would be a great time to get some shots with a camera crew."

"Excellent! Mercedes, the station was mighty pleased with your work on the last piece. We got a ton of feedback from folks. If everything goes right, this might be a steady gig for you if you're interested. I'm sending Gabrielle and Frank down first thing in the morning. They should arrive around nine."

"Great. Tell them to meet me at the church, and we will go from there." Mercedes hung up with Reggie, and excitement began to build inside her. It wasn't excitement about another gig, though; this was something bigger. This was going to save Grant's job at the church.

"What is it?" Grant asked.

"You need to call Harold and Chase. We are going to do another story."

"Another news story? About Shady Springs?" Grant stared at Mercedes with obvious confusion.

"Yes, tell them to meet us here at the diner as soon as possible." Ideas formed in Mercedes' mind. She didn't know if her news story would be enough to change the mind of the councilmen, but she was going to try.

Chase and Harold were at the diner in less than ten minutes. Mercedes told them about the exposé the station wanted to do about Shady Springs.

"I still don't understand how this can change anything," Grant said.

"Do you really think the deacons want the world to know how they've outed their pastor because their beloved cloud disappeared?" Mercedes asked.

"Yeah, but isn't this like blackmail or something? I mean, I want to stay but because people want me here, not because people feel threatened."

"But people do want you here!" Alice chimed in and began to cry. "I want you here; Mom does; Harold and Chase do . . ." She sniffed and wiped her eyes.

"Okay, that's four people, sis," Grant said softly.

"There's a whole lot more than that." Gladys walked up to the table with her posse and joined the conversation.

"That's right," the other ladies murmured.

"So, what do we need to do to get this ball rolling?" Gladys demanded. "Sorry, I couldn't help overhearing your conversation."

"Sure, you couldn't help it." Chase rolled his eyes.

"You ladies need to get started on the thing you do best," Harold said with a twinkle in his eye.

"What's that?" a white-haired lady spoke up behind Gladys timidly.

"Start making some phone calls—to everyone. Tell them there's going to be another story about Shady Springs. But tell them you are afraid the news is going to convey we are getting rid of our pastor."

Grant covered his ears. "I'm not hearing this." He shook his head. "Ladies, please don't . . ." His voice trailed off as they fluttered like a flock of geese through the diner door. Grant questioned Harold and Chase, "I thought we didn't want things to get ugly?"

"It has to get ugly before it gets pretty," Darlene said as she began to take their plates.

Everyone turned to her in surprise.

"Nicholas Sparks," Darlene said with a shrug.

"Should we wait until the council members catch wind, or do you think we should call them?" Chase asked.

"Give it a few minutes . . ." Harold advised.

Harold's and Chase's phones rang simultaneously.

"Here we go," Chase said with raised eyebrows to Harold while answering his phone.

Grant pulled Mercedes aside out of the booth. "I understand what you're trying to do, and I appreciate it, truly. I can't have the congregation getting hurt by this, though, Mercedes. I don't want to lose any of my new converts."

"Grant, I promise I'm not going to report anything negative about the church or the town. The Lord may have given me this opportunity just for this occasion. I have to at least try!"

Alice approached them. "Grant, can you bring Mercedes to the house? I'm going to go home and take Mom her dinner. She's gonna want to know everything that has happened." Alice gave them both a quick hug. "Thank you," she whispered in Mercedes' ear.

"Don't thank me yet," Mercedes whispered back. "Just keep praying."

Harold and Chase came over to them as Alice left. "Special board meeting has been called. We'll let you know what's been decided," Chase said.

"Alright, thanks, guys." Grant gave them both a hug.

Grant seemed lost in thought on the ride back to his mom's house, and Mercedes worried she might have overstepped. "Are you upset with me?"

"What? No, not at all. Just a lot to think about."

"Okay," Mercedes said, still unsure. She and Grant had been texting and calling each other almost every day since she left. He had mentioned coming down to meet her family later in the month. She really liked him and didn't want this to damage their relationship. "If you want me to cancel the story, I will. The station may send another person, though, to cover it."

Grant looked at her in alarm. "No, Mercedes. I could never ask you to do that." He took her hand and squeezed it.

"Plus, I'd have to sway another reporter," he said jokingly.

Mercedes laughed. "I don't know what I want to do about my job, Grant. If Reggie does offer me a reporter gig, it could mean a lot of traveling."

"Is traveling something you are interested in?"

"It could be fun. But it's not my passion. I really love studying the weather."

"I would keep praying for the right job, then. When the right door opens, things will fall into place. You didn't get any leads when you went home to your mom's?"

"No, not really. To be honest, my focus was more on dealing with some things that I had been struggling with."

Grant tilted his head. "Like what?"

She hesitated. "I let some people—people in our church—hurt me years ago. I didn't deal with it, and it made me a little bitter with the church and God."

Mercedes played with the cuff on her sleeve. "Anyhow, I talked with my pastor about it, and I made peace with everything—and forgiveness."

"That's awesome, Mercedes. I know that must have been difficult to do."

"Believe me," Mercedes said with a laugh. "It was way more difficult carrying around all that extra baggage for what, five years?"

Grant nodded. "I don't know how people manage their whole lives carrying around past hurt. It's an awful weight to bear. I'm so thankful I can give whatever it is to God."

"Yeah. It's been a relief to let it all go."

Grant pulled his truck into his childhood home's driveway. It was a plain white house except for some colorful gnomes. Carol started a collection of gnomes when Grant was younger, and now, they fully lined her sidewalk.

"Are you coming in?" Mercedes asked softly.

"Just for a bit. I still need to go over my sermon notes. It feels so weird. This will be my last night sleeping at the parsonage."

Mercedes noticed the tired lines around his eyes. "It doesn't look like you've been getting much sleep lately."

"I haven't," he confessed. "It's not that I'm worried about myself as much but for my people— what will happen to them when I'm gone? Then, of course, there's you."

"Me?" Mercedes leaned back in surprise. "What about me?"

Grant twisted his college ring around his finger. "I worry that you might take a job far away, and I won't be able to see you. I worry that life in the ministry isn't what you want. I know we've only known each other a few weeks, but I feel like what we have is special. I haven't felt like this over someone in a long time. I was engaged four years ago. Her name was Natalie, Nat for short. She drove home from Bible college late one night with some friends. A big rig lost control, and they were all killed. I threw all my effort and energy into my studies and the ministry. I didn't want to pursue a relationship with anyone. When you came to Shady Springs, you changed all of that for me, Mercedes. I finally feel like I can move on, that I can love again."

Mercedes bit her lower lip. Her heart ached for his loss. She hated that he stressed about their relationship on top of everything else he was dealing with. She placed her hand on top of his. "Grant, I feel the same way about you. If you had asked me a couple of weeks ago about ministry or church, I probably would have laughed at you. But since I've been working on forgiving others and forgiving myself, I have peace about whatever God's will is for my life." She met his gaze, filled with adoration for her. She whispered, "And I hope and pray it includes you."

The next morning, Mercedes woke up somewhat discouraged. She had received a text from Grant during the night that the board didn't reverse their decision. She'd been so sure God was going to use her story to change their minds. *You know, Lord, I'm not giving up. I believe You can change this around if you want. Please be with Grant today; give him strength and wisdom and guide his words. Be with the Shady Springs congregation and the council today. Let everything be done for Your*

glory. She slipped on a simple cobalt blue knot dress with three-quarter length sleeves and finished getting ready.

When she entered the kitchen, Carol and Alice were both dressed. They were sitting at the table with platters of crisp bacon and scrambled eggs. Carol wore a navy and white sundress, while Alice wore a pencil dress with a pastel floral print. The morning sunlight came through the kitchen window, depicting a quintessential Sunday morning breakfast in the South. They were pretty as a card despite the glum expressions on their faces.

"Morning. I guess you heard about the board's decision," Mercedes said as she slid into a chair.

"Yes. I have to admit I'm disappointed, but if it's the Lord's will, I know it will be okay. We will be okay," Carol said with a small smile.

"I have a feeling it's not over. I'm not giving up yet." Mercedes tilted her chin up.

Carol smiled at her. "I guess we will find out soon enough. I hope you're right."

"Would you like some bacon and eggs? Coffee?" Alice asked.

"Sure." Mercedes started to rise.

"Oh, don't get up. I got you. I love your dress." Alice waved her off as she poured a cup of coffee and handed it to her.

"Thanks." Mercedes breathed in the aroma.

"Do you have a lot to prepare for to get ready for your story?" Carol asked.

"I organized some thoughts last night. The only things left to do are to shoot some footage and do a few interviews. I'm going to head over after I eat. My crew should be arriving soon."

"There's our star reporter!" Gabrielle hugged Mercedes as Frank got the rest of the equipment out of the news van.

"It's so good to see you again," Mercedes said with a smile. "Shouldn't we help Frank unload?"

"No way, girl. We had a bet going, and he lost."

Mercedes laughed as Frank made a face at Gabrielle behind her back. "Do I want to know what the bet was about?"

"Nah, probably not," Gabrielle gave her a wink.

"So, what's going on here?" Frank said as he leaned on Mercedes, trying to catch his breath.

"Geez, Frank. You really do need to start working out," Gabriele chided.

Ignoring the comment, Frank turned to Mercedes. "Come on, what's the story?"

"Today, the church is having a celebration service for their current pastor—"

"You mean Grant, the hottie?" Gabrielle interrupted.

"Oh, is that your nickname for me?" A familiar voice spoke from behind them.

Mercedes could feel the heat rise to her temple. She gave Gabrielle a pleading look.

"Sorry, Mercedes." Gabrielle shrugged with a smile.

Mercedes slowly turned to see Grant grinning broadly. She covered her forehead with her hand and closed her eyes. "Anyway, they are going to have a special service and picnic for Grant in honor of his last Sunday."

"Wait. Why is it his last Sunday? Is the church closing?" Frank asked.

"The church isn't closing. They are looking for a new pastor," Mercedes said diplomatically.

Frank frowned. "Well, let's get started."

After they filmed scenes of the lake and the church, it was time for the service to start.

The congregation filled every pew inside the church. Harold and Grant brought over some chairs from the fellowship hall, but there were still people standing in the back. Mercedes leaned over to Carol and gestured behind her. "Are all of these people members here at Shady Springs?"

"No, a lot of them are just nosy town members," Alice retorted loudly.

"Alice." Carol admonished her daughter with a look.

After a few opening songs, Grant stood to preach. Mercedes could feel tears beginning to well up as she realized the finality of everything. This was his last time to stand behind this pulpit. She glanced over at his mom and sister, and they already had a box of tissue. Alice gave her a knowing smile and handed her one.

"I know you all are expecting a sermon from me this morning," Grant began, "but I had a few members of our congregation approach me about giving their testimony today. As Christians, we are known by our fruit, and I can't think of a better way to leave than seeing fruit the Lord has allowed me to bear. I am so proud of what you guys are doing for the Lord, and I love you all dearly. I believe Gertie is going to speak first."

Mercedes turned to Alice and Carol and whispered, "Did y'all know about this?"

Alice whispered back, "I think it was last minute. I saw Gertie talking to him before the service."

Mercedes felt a nudge of guilt. She hadn't spoken with Gertie since she checked out of the B&B. Gertie hadn't been with Gladys and the other ladies at the diner last night. Later in the evening, she asked Grant about her and Bertie. Bertie had been screened for neurodegenerative disorders and was admitted to a hospital. Thankfully, it looked like there wasn't going to be a trial. Grant said Gertie was doing the best she could.

"I just wanted to say what a blessing Pastor Grant has been to me. I've been in church my whole life, and I can tell you I've grown more under his ministry than any other preacher I've known. When my husband went on to glory, Pastor Grant was there. When I had trouble with my sister, he was there to help and pray and offer guidance. All the things a great pastor does. Thank you so much for your service to our town. I am so proud to call you my pastor." Gertie looked at him with teary eyes and chuckled. "Whew! I did it without blubbering!"

Grant gave her a heartfelt hug and helped her down as Gladys made her way to the front.

This should be interesting, Mercedes thought.

Gladys moved the microphone closer to her mouth and cleared her throat. "Pastor Grant has always made me feel like I had a special part in our church. I know some people think I'm a silly, old woman that often sticks her foot in her mouth."

A coughing sound came from behind her, and Mercedes knew that it had to be Harold or Chase.

Gladys continued unphased, "Some may think the flower arrangements and decorations are trivial, but Pastor Grant has always made me feel like my contributions were important. He values the young and the old in our church, which is sometimes missing in other places. I just want to publicly say how thankful I am to be a part of his ministry."

"Thank you, Gladys," Grant said, and she gave him a hug.

After Gladys spoke, Harold, Chase, and some of the youth gave testimonies.

When it seemed like the service drew to an end, Grant took the pulpit again. "I just want to say thank you one more time for allowing me to serve God here in Shady Springs—"

"Wait, Pastor Grant. I have something to say."

Mercedes turned around, surprised to see Derek Rossi standing.

"Alright, Derek. Come on up." Grant moved aside for Derek to take the podium.

"I, uh, just wanted to say that—well, if it wasn't for Pastor Grant's ministry here, I don't know where I'd be. I'm not good at speakin' like this, so I'm going to be quick. I discovered this past month that I need a better relationship with Christ. And I came to that conclusion by watching this man. You can tell that Pastor Grant has a real connection with Christ. He lives what he preaches. I mean, he's not perfect, of course, but he does his best to honor what the Bible says. I'm just thankful God used Pastor Grant to show me this before I did anything I'd regret. I wish he could stay so I could learn more." Derek turned to Grant. "Thanks, man."

"Thanks, Derek. I appreciate that." Grant turned to his congregation. "Okay, well, I know everybody is eager to eat—"

"Wait, Pastor Grant!" A gruff voice came from the back.

Mercedes turned to see who was calling out. She couldn't believe her eyes to see Elder Harper. He still looked as cantankerous as the first time she interviewed him. He glowered over the people in the pew in front of him as he stood in his tweed dark brown suit.

Grant seemed taken back as well. "Elder Harper, come ahead."

"I'm not gonna walk all the way up there. That would take too long for what I have to say. Pastor Grant, I wasn't happy when you took our pastorate. You were young and inexperienced. I didn't think you were worthy of our church or our congregation."

Elder Harper's wife tugged at him to sit down.

Mercedes sat shocked as Grant's face began to flush, and his knuckles whitened around the pulpit.

"Hang on. I'm going somewhere with this." He shooed his wife's hand away. "Anyway, I know I've been a thorn in your side since the day you came. I used the cloud leaving us as a reason to get rid of you. But I got to thinking as all these people talked about your influence in their lives—that when the children of Israel lost their pillar of cloud, they didn't run Joshua out of camp. And well, I'm wrong to run you out of this church. I'm sorry it's taken me so long to realize it."

Chase stood and gaped at the old man. "Can you say that again, Harper? I suppose it's better late than never. We need that on record. Where's our church secretary?"

Elder Harper threw his hands in the air. "All right. I'm wrong, and I'm sorry. Can you forgive me? And will you please stay and be our pastor?"

Mercedes almost couldn't believe what unfolded in front of her. *Thank you, Lord! I see You! Thank You for this miracle!* Everyone was crying. Alice and Carol were hugging. Grant walked down and hugged Elder Harper. Gladys was trying to hug Harold. This was more miraculous than being led by a cloud. This was God changing the heart of man. All they needed was a wisp of faith. Mercedes couldn't wait to see what the Lord would do next.

REFLECTION QUESTIONS

1. Mercedes' life plan, her dream, and her career were taken away. Can you think of a time in your life when you had to tear up your script or when things didn't go the way you planned?

2. We see how God placed certain people in Grant's life to guide him. Who has God placed in your life to aid you? Or instead, for you to guide them?

3. Oftentimes, fear of failure, rejection, or humiliation keeps us from moving forward in faith. What fear is keeping you from moving forward?

4. Do you think God can still perform miracles today like the way he led Pastor Ford with the cloud?

5. Lois Rosteller had moments when it seemed like he had conquered his personal demons. What were the moments where he let them overtake him?

6. Mercedes had a hard time letting go of past hurts from church people. Her parents actually went to the ones who hurt their family, which goes in line with Matthew 18:15 (KJV): "Moreover if thy brother shall trespass against thee, go and tell him his fault between thee and him alone." This is a struggle for many. What benefits do you see happening by following this verse?

7. Elder Harper was able to reconcile with Pastor Grant. If that reconciliation had not taken place and Grant still had to leave Shady Springs, how could God have worked that out for good?

8. When in your life have things not gone as you expected, only to see how God was leading you down a better path?

ACKNOWLEDGMENTS

I would like to first thank the Lord for giving me the inspiration and the courage to write this book.

Thank you to my mom and dad, who kept urging me to write and create.

To my husband, Lee, for indulging me in bringing *A Wisp of Faith* into fruition and not "eye-roll" when I talk about future writing projects.

To my children for letting me have my writing time.

To all my students for inspiring me to follow my dreams.

To all my friends and family who have given encouragement along the way.

To Kary Oberbrunner and the amazing author coaches at Author Academy Elite, the Igniting Souls Tribe, and my editors at The Guild.

A very special thanks to the following few. Thank you so much for being a part of the *A Wisp of Faith* project.

Lexi Birmingham for graciously giving your insight on the field of meteorology.

Michael Metts and Karen Weido for your valuable input as beta readers.

Daniel Medina, Jane Stephen, Bee Persaud, Amy Beasley, Carrie Jenkins, Clara Anders, Jessica Moore, Lee Gilkey, Mary McBeath, James and Mary Pepper, Patti Vickery, and the Homeless No More Ministry.

ABOUT THE AUTHOR

A Texas girl born and raised, Chrystal J. Gilkey resides in El Dorado, Arkansas, with her husband, three children, and two cats. A passionate coffee and tea drinker, Chrystal enjoys playing the piano, reading, and gardening. One day, she dreams of owning a pet minipig.

Chrystal was reminded of her love of writing after she was awarded a grant she wrote for her school. She hopes this book serves as a testament to her students that their dreams are reachable. Chrystal writes to encourage and strengthen people's faith in God.

For more encouragement and inspiration, you can find Chrystal on Facebook, Twitter, Instagram, and LinkedIn @chrystaljgilkey.

Let's Connect!

Speaking and writing to encourage & inspire!

CHRYSTALJGILKEY.COM

YOU'VE SEEN THE CLOUD.
ARE YOU READY TO GRAB HOLD?

A Wisp of Faith

HELP OUT OF THE HURT

THE FORECAST

REMEMBERANCE

FORGIVENESS

OBEDIENCE

CONFIDENCE